SHADOW OF A HANG ROPE

OTHER FIVE STAR WESTERN TITLES BY LAURAN PAINE:

Tears of the Heart (1995); *Lockwood* (1996); *The White Bird* (1997); *The Grand Ones of San Ildefonso* (1997); *Cache Cañon* (1998); *The Killer Gun* (1998); *The Mustangers* (1999); *The Running Iron* (2000); *The Dark Trail* (2001); *Guns in the Desert* (2002); *Gathering Storm* (2003); *Night of the Comancheros* (2003); *Rain Valley* (2004); *Guns in Oregon* (2004); *Holding the Ace Card* (2005); *Feud on the Mesa* (2005); *Gunman* (2006); *The Plains of Laramie* (2006); *Halfmoon Ranch* (2007); *Man from Durango* (2007); *The Quiet Gun* (2008); *Patterson* (2008); *Hurd's Crossing* (2008); *Rangers of El Paso* (2009); *Sheriff of Hangtown* (2009); *Gunman's Moon* (2009); *Promise of Revenge* (2010); *Kansas Kid* (2010); *Guns of Thunder* (2010); *Iron Marshal* (2011); *Prairie Town* (2011); *The Last Gun* (2011); *Man Behind the Gun* (2012); *Lightning Strike* (2012); *The Drifter* (2012); *The Texan Rides Alone* (2013); *The Story of Buckhorn* (2013)

SHADOW OF A HANG ROPE

A WESTERN STORY

LAURAN PAINE

FIVE STAR

A part of Gale, Cengage Learning

GALE
CENGAGE Learning®

Farmington Hills, Mich • San Francisco • New York • Waterville, Maine
Meriden, Conn • Mason, Ohio • Chicago

GALE
CENGAGE Learning·

LIBRARY OF CONGRESS CATALOGING-IN-PUBLICATION DATA

Paine, Lauran.
   Shadow of a hang rope : a western story / by Lauran Paine.
  — First edition.
    pages cm
   ISBN 978-1-4328-2770-0 (hardcover) — ISBN 1-4328-2770-7
(hardcover)
   I. Title.
PS3566.A34S35 2014
813'.54—dc23   2014003142

First Edition. First Printing: June 2014
Published in conjunction with Golden West Literary Agency.
Find us on Facebook– https://www.facebook.com/FiveStarCengage
Visit our website– http://www.gale.cengage.com/fivestar/
Contact Five Star™ Publishing at FiveStar@cengage.com

Printed in the United States of America
1 2 3 4 5 6 7 18 17 16 15 14

SHADOW OF A HANG ROPE

CHAPTER ONE

The day was new, as yet unmarked by men, and though its saffron light with the chill of dawn lay clearly upon the land, the man in the small restaurant couldn't see the bottom of his empty coffee cup because of indoor shadows.

Vacaville was hushed with shrouding stillness. The unkempt rider swiveled upon his bench and gazed outward, where rows of slumbering buildings were soft-cast and peaceful in the murky light. A Land Office, a mercantile, a livery barn with awakening flies, a yawning swamper leaning upon a bristly broom who explored his inner mouth and spat, welcoming the dawn that way. A bank with high-barred windows and the stiff appearance of banks.

The rider turned when a voice spoke, gazed upward, and shook his head, unwilling to break the spell of hurting beauty. No more coffee, thanks. He made a cigarette with fingers working like hairless spiders, lit it, and exhaled.

Unemployed with $100, the outriding job ending at Vacaville, he sat now wholly relaxed, blood thick and sluggish, objectively detached, listening to the whisper in his mind that told him he was again at trail's end. Years of starts and stops trouped past, days of sparkling sun and gritty gray, times of hurry and delay, of laughter and pain, of drifting always with his perfect gift of youth, spending a legacy of size and strength without care or thought until now, in the sallow shadows of an all-night café at Vacaville, Arizona Territory. He was slouched beneath his dust-furred big hat, watching nothing and feeling its intangible beauty—$100, twenty-nine years of living, in the midst of nothing.

Two men entered the café, passed him unseeingly, dropped down, and hunched over the counter, holstered guns dangling against the wooden bench, voices low, eyes still with cold thoughtfulness devoid of feeling, of consciousness of things that were, like the merging colors or the lone man nearby looking into nothing, which was, of course, his future. He heard their voices order ham and eggs and coffee. He heard the clatter of plates and smelled the sullen grease and a word came through occasionally, jarringly, to foul the stillness and the melancholy freshness of a time before the burning sun arose.

"A hundred dollars in advance."

"Where?"

"Hunter's Spring."

"With the horses?"

"A bill of sale. Don't forget that, understand?"

"Yes. When's he get the balance?"

Words that dulled and died unimportantly. The man under the black hat got up with a sigh and walked across the room, out into the new day barely remembering, but inwardly his mind said: *There, see how men make money when they've got a hundred dollars? Not you. You'll spend your hundred for things you don't need, things you can't hold, things that evaporate.*

The sun jumped over the saw-tooth mountains like a seed popped out of a grape. Hung high, pouring a swath of burning light that scalded gargantuan tunnels through the veils of saffron mist, trampling, running, expanding until the gentler light was flooded over, smothered, extinguished. July 13th 1877, in Vacaville, Arizona Territory.

He watched people appear through a slanting expression that was near smiling, near irony. The thick saddler unlocking his door, motioning at the flies before he opened it, disappearing inside where horse sweat and man sweat and leather smell merged in a pleasant world of dinginess.

The man with the big cigar, symbol of absolutism, stalking the swamper leaning on the bristly broom, bringing him out of his curl of lethargy with a tobacco-scented bark, savoring his employee's secret guilt at being caught standing still. Brushing past with regal stride, entering a fly-specked cubicle that was office and whipping room to a livery barn owner.

And a girl as fresh as the dawn that had now died, leading a lame horse across the dust of the roadway, dark hair catching light, imprisoning it, golden flesh of flawless, retroussé profile, leaving an impression under the motionless man's heart, stirring a longing he had no right to, an impression worth many times $100.

So he crossed aimlessly to the overnight corral and saw that his horse had been fed. Dumb brute eyes gazed through the cribbed poles at him with liquid poignancy, as though his animal could pity the man, and voices spanked the sunshine from around in back of the barn where the farrier had his black and tumbled shop and raised sleek flies off hoof parings.

". . . when I went out to feed him this morning."

A cranky voice, uncleared and bubbling, said: "Well, it ain't the shoe, I'll tell you that. Maybe a tendon. Too much jamming, maybe."

The girl's tone grew quickly sharp. "That's impossible. I don't ride him hard."

The disagreeable man's voice said: "He's lame, anyway." There was the flat sound of expectoration. "Tie him outside, and when I get around to it, I'll look at him."

The man in the black hat turned slowly, knowing she would be walking away. The same profile, only closer. He thought that all girls have beauty, but its quality differs. This was finest quality, a shade of song-poem beauty. In movement, in carriage—in everything.

She stopped on the plank walk and smiled up at a man. They spoke and she went on, but the stranger by the corral didn't follow her with his half-smiling half-ironic eyes, he looked after the man. Dark blood moved. An iron fingernail was drawn across the pink moistness of his mind. It hurt. $100!

The liveryman came up genially and his eyes more than his mouth said: "Going to leave him here all day . . . be another half dollar."

The rider dug it out of his pants pocket and handed it over wordlessly. The cigar bobbed thanks. The man was turning.

"There was a girl brought a brown horse around back here a minute ago . . . what's her name?"

The cigar came back part way. Behind it bright eyes sharpened in their smallness. They knew a drifter like they knew an outlaw. "Her? Girl with dark hair? That's Joyce Porter, Judge Porter's daughter."

"Thanks."

The heat increased, danced its macabre shimmy, sucked in and blew out, flattened and distorted distances, laying heavily across the rider's shoulders and digging into his covered flesh. He went into the shade near the blacksmith shop and dropped down there. $100. What would it be like to own such a girl? The illness of knowing too much beauty drained him more than the sun. Other men had women like that. *Other men had more than a hundred dollars, too!* He picked up a stone and gripped it. The edges bruised. They cut. He squeezed it tighter and self-hate made the pain insignificant. Twenty-nine and a lousy $100.

The big fist opened, the stone fell, shone with curdling scarlet. He wiped the blood off on his pants. Sleek flies came out of nowhere, by instinct, by scent.

The dead cigarette hung from his mouth and his eyes lay

against the far-away range and very slowly a crazy idea took shape, grew, and became irresponsibly substantial. Then he spat out the cigarette, knowing that just a girl walking by a man like that could make an outlaw out of him for life, could get a man in a big black hat hanged. Or her memory could wrench a drifter out of doldrums and force him to risk, lose or win. And if he won, could a judge named Porter turn aside from a moneyed man named John Hawk?

When the farrier came out, he cast a surly glance at the slumped figure, then bent to examine the brown horse. The rider got up, dusted off his breeches and walked closer.

"Where's a place called Hunter's Spring?"

"East of town about twelve miles."

"On a road?"

"Stage road. It's marked."

"Thanks."

"Uhn-huh."

The rider contemplated the doubled-over form a moment, then smiled in a crooked way and went to the livery barn, caught his horse, saddled up, and rode eastward out of Vacaville on the stage road.

It was crazy. Who was supposed to be there and wouldn't he know John Hawk from the cowboy in the café? And his mind said, with an unseen yawn: *Scared of risk. You'd never risk. If you lose the damned hundred dollars, what of it. You'd lose it anyway, wouldn't you?*

He smiled into the burnished desert and felt its singing voice come out from under scalded rocks. But horse thieves have ways of losing lives as well as $100. Risk, high odds. The alternative—riding, drifting, tumbling, an autumn leaf, $100 now and then. No risk—no nothing. Pay $100 to make a man an outlaw, a horse thief—maybe a dead man, $100 for a herd of somebody's horses. Sell them and keep on moving.

11

A warped skein of thrill came to life that had always been a part of him anyway. Easy for a man to turn outlaw. Just a girl walking. . . .

Hunter's Spring was a sump where coyote and deer tracks were embedded in stinking clay and green slime formed a necklace of seepage of the dark water. He had no trouble finding it, for once an unknown hand had cut the name with terrible disappointment into a sandstone upthrust. A fist driven by despair at sight and smell of the nearest water in this land of eternal thirst. Carved it with hatred and finality. Hunter's Spring. Left unsaid: dead water, a sump of scum.

John Hawk stood in the pale shade, knowing he could see movement a long time before he was seen. And he waited. Counted the $100, looked gravely into the cylinder of his pistol, thought of a golden girl walking, and waited.

Then, when a furl of dust appeared northward fear flooded upward, clogging his throat; guilt increased the dryness of his mouth. Sweat ran under his clothing. Then the dust stopped, hung far out like a ragged fist and began to settle. A lone horseman emerged from it, jogging slowly down the weaving land.

Well, $100. . . .

"Howdy."

John Hawk stood loosely. He nodded. "Howdy. Pretty hot."

The rider sat there, gazing downward out of a pinched-up face, neither evil nor saintly. The face of man sculpted from a life of hardship, peril. "Hot enough. Like the hubs of hell." The horseman continued to gaze out of small, grating eyes. "You alone?"

"Yes."

"Just passing through?"

"No, I've got a hundred dollars in my pocket."

The long stare became knowing. "Oh," the man said, that and no more.

"You want it?"

A flicker of the little eyes. "Always got use for a hundred dollars."

"It's yours for a bill of sale."

"Bill of sale?"

"For the horses you brought." John Hawk thrust his chin in the direction of the dying dust devil.

The rider swung out and down and grinned and shook his head. "Cagey, aren't you? Well, it's a good way to be. Me, too." He trickled reins through his fingers. "Where's old Smalley?"

John shrugged. Horse, man, or dog? "Pretty hot for riding," he murmured, and the other man laughed thinly and went over into the shade.

"All right." He squatted, pushed his hat far back, and groped for a pencil, a piece of paper. He spoke as he made large, oval letters in an unpracticed hand. "Tell Smalley I want the rest when I get back from Sonora."

"I'll tell him."

"Know what to do with the horses?"

"Sure," John lied.

A sigh. "Here, this'll make it legal as all hell." And the man laughed.

John counted out the money. A claw closed around it, crammed it into pants pockets. "Christ, I wouldn't do that again for ten thousand. Not in weather like this." Little eyes swung around and showed their core of toughness. "Sixty head of good broke stock is hell to push into a desert this time of the year. Keep trying to bust back. Well"—he was trickling the reins again—"I'll be back when it cools off. Tell him, will you? Tell him I'll hunt him up in Vacaville maybe next month, maybe the month after."

"I'll tell him."

"S'long then."

John watched him jog southward with heat waves making it appear that he rode six inches above the ground and not upon it.

The sixty-odd horses were tail-tucked, weary. He bunched them up and started aimlessly westward, skirting the outpost ranches. Beyond acquisition he had not planned. It had seemed implausible he would get this far.

He pushed them hard until rib cages heaved and their coats were flecked with sudsy crust. Drove them into the evening before he cooled them out at slower gaits. Rode with them until a lop-sided moon showed and kept them going until it was high, then stopped in a bronco-grass swale and turned his saddle blanket over and let his own horse carry the uncinched saddle, grazing among them with reins dragging.

He looked up at the sky and smiled. Sixty head of good horses for $100. A trader would pay $600 for the lot. He lay back, a horse thief for $500 profit. For the risk, $500 he could do something with. What? He heard the horses eating. Something. . . .

When dawn came John Hawk, horse thief, was far over the land with a guttering tangle of dust behind him. He kept the horses moving fast until he came to a river. That stop was too long but the animals needed it. On again under a less lop-sided moon. Four days of it and he was nearing a town. A place he'd remembered.

A meeting was effected without effort, the bill of sale transferred, the gaunt horses corralled, money taken. He rode back out a ways and spent the night upon the desert and before dawn was riding again—eastward, back the way he'd come. Because of the walk of a girl.

In a heat-hazed nooning spot, he lay beneath a flecked patch of shade and watched a red-tailed hawk spin in artful circles, tight and predatory, near some bluffs that rose up like ramparts of a giant's fortress. And there were fleecy clouds as voluptuous as sin, building up in irresistible formations. He let the sweat dry on his skin, the shade flood over him. He slept.

Vacaville was sweltering as always when he scuffled through its roadway dust. Peril lay in its drabness, the sunburned warpedness in the blank faces he saw by the dozens, but the lost sliver of metal that he was had been sucked back by a magnetism, and if a twining thread of uneasiness was in him, it didn't show.

He put up his horse in the outside corral as he'd done before and went over to the farrier's shop. The farrier was as always surly, seamed face deep with coal dust, bitter. And John Hawk smiled as amiably as a fed puppy.

"I've got a big bay horse over in the corral that needs new shoes all around. Branded PW Diamond on the left shoulder."

"I'm busier'n a bitch wolf at whelping time," the farrier said disagreeably.

"All right," Hawk said pleasantly. "Show me where the tools are and I'll do it, and pay you half price."

The blacksmith straightened up, studied him boldly, acidly. "I suppose you're a horse-shoer, too," he said.

Still smiling, John Hawk answered: "As good as most and better'n some. Want to see?"

The farrier grew still straighter. His gray eyes were like bleached dung and yet they were curious, too. "Yeah," he said, "I'd like to see. If you're any good, I'll hire you."

"Have trouble with your help?"

"Trouble. Trouble's not the word for it. None of 'em is worth much at their best."

"Then," John said pleasantly, "it isn't them, it's you. Where are the tools?"

A rusty color hung around the farrier's downward mouth,

15

drawn tight and belligerent-looking. He didn't answer, only gestured.

John got his horse and stripped off his shirt, his only shirt, hung up his hat and gun belt, put on a shiny mule-skin apron, and went to work. The sleek flies came daintily to explore his ears while both hands were occupied and sweat gushed. He worked slowly, deliberately, and when he was doing the final rasping, the farrier came over and stumped completely around his big bay horse, looking.

"I thought you were a cowboy," he said, "and all cowboys know all there is to know. Ever work in a shop?"

"For two winters, about six, eight years ago."

"What'd they pay you?"

Without looking up, John said: "About half what shops pay nowadays."

"Humph!"

John dropped the last hoof, threw the rasp into the tool bucket, tossed his head to fling off sweat, removed the apron, rolled it, and dropped it into the bucket, also. He was flush-faced. "How much do I owe you?"

"Dollar. Want a job?"

A slow wag of the head. "Nope. Someday my stomach would be sour the same way yours was and you'd fire me after I'd crammed your head into a water bucket. Where's the wash trough?"

He held out the money. The farrier made no move to take it. Instead his stumpy cigar grew rigid, his antagonistic eyes colder. "Smart, aren't you? When I was your age, I'd've kicked a sight of pudding out of you for that lip."

"Naw, you wouldn't have," John said. "Not then or now. Tell me something. What was wrong with Joyce Porter's brown horse a week or so ago when she brought it over here limping?"

"Nothing, not a cussed thing."

"Just limped because one leg was tired, huh?"

The farrier took the silver dollar, pocketed it, and jerked a thumb toward the heat waves beyond the doorway. "Out," he said, and went back to his forge, red-necked and brittle-stepping.

John washed and dressed, led his horse back to the livery barn, stopped in the smashing yellow brilliance of the public corral, turned, and went into the cool, dark barn. "Here," he said to the swamper, "put him in a stall, give him a bath and hay, and grain him."

"Dollar a day inside," the swamper said. "The others are extras."

John gave the man five silver dollars. The big coins were surprisingly cool in his hand. Impersonally cool, he thought. They had no eyes, no memories, which was just as well.

Then he went out the front door, crossed the roadway with an absorbed air, went down the alley he'd seen Judge Porter's daughter emerge from with her lame horse, and plunged deep into its protected shadows.

Finding the house was easy because he recognized the brown horse. He went to the fence and leaned over it for a moment, then entered through the gate, walked to the back stoop, up three wooden steps to the door, and knocked.

A black woman opened the door and squinted up into his face. "Yas, suh?"

"Miss Porter."

"I'll fetch her."

Prickles of something like heat rash, only it wasn't, crinkled his scalp. When she finally appeared, he was losing his nerve.

"Yes?"

"The blacksmith across the way told me your horse was lame and he didn't know what caused it. He sort of hinted that I might be able to help you. . . ."

17

Her hazel eyes widened. "Sean O'Brien?" she said in surprise. "That's unusual for him. Well, my horse seems to be all right now, though. Still, if you'd care to look. . . ."

She swept past him and down the little steps. He watched her go a moment before he paced after her. She turned at the iron gate, leading into the horse lot, where a shed made a slanting, triangular splotch of diluted shade.

"Are you a veterinarian?"

"No," he said, moving closer, bending a little to grasp the latch, "just a horseman." Then grinning at some private humor of his own, he added: "A professional horseman, Miss Porter."

"Well. . . ."

"After you, ma'am."

The brown horse watched them with languid interest until they were close, then ambled toward the shed and its shade. John stood still, watching him move away, then he followed the girl into the coolness.

"He isn't limping now, ma'am," he said.

"No, it was just that one day, you see."

"Uhn-huh. Did you do anything for him?"

"I cleaned his hoofs."

"Find anything? A stone bruise or anything like that?"

"No." She was watching his face, seeing it thoughtful and pensive, red from some recent exertion. More pleasant and open-looking than handsome.

"Do you happen to know what a hoof felon is, ma'am?"

"I don't believe so," she said, returning her gaze to the horse.

"It works like this. If the sole gets badly bruised, the horse may only limp a day or two, then act normal, but the felon growth keeps getting bigger, inside the hoof you see, until it breaks out into a big running sore. Now, this time of the year. . . ."

"Do you think he might have a hoof felon? How can you tell?"

"There's really only one sure way to tell," John said without looking away from the horse. "Use him. Ride him for a few miles over rough ground. If there's an internal felon, it'll show up then."

"Oh."

He laid a detached glance upon her. "He looks like a pet."

"He's a very good saddle animal," she said, balancing some inner thought of her own, speaking slowly. "But I wouldn't want him to be lame even if he wasn't."

"Well," John said, "if you'll saddle him up, I'll go get my horse and you can show me where there's some rough ground, because I'm a stranger hereabouts, and we'll see if he's got a hoof felon."

She stared fixedly at the brown horse's near front leg. "That's awfully kind of you but. . . ."

"Oh, I suppose you might say that I owe Sean O'Brien that much."

She looked upward. "Are you a friend of his?"

The half-amused, half-ironic smile showed. "If he has any friends at all," John said dryly, "I reckon you could call me one."

And they both laughed at that.

"All right, but I don't feel that I should put you out like this."

He was moving toward the gate, reddened face looking redder. "It won't take long. I'll get my horse."

He saddled up in the gloom of the shadowy livery barn by instinct, eyes glued to the fly-specked wall without seeing it. Where did ideas like that come from? Where does that kind of nerve dwell in a man for almost thirty years, fed and nurtured yet hidden, and coming up in him so late? He gave the latigo a final flip, swung into the saddle, and turned the big bay horse.

The same place the insanity lurks in a man that makes him steal sixty head of horses, then return to the country where he stole them. Where? He had no idea. Why? Because of the walk of a girl.

They rode north out of town. He followed her, reining easterly a little, and the burning sun turned her flesh golden, her dark hair lighter with gold deep in its masses. And she looked squarely at him.

"Should it be rocky ground, Mister . . . ?"

"John Hawk. Yes, rocky ground would be fine. But hilly country with trees would probably be better," he said, because it was hotter than the inside of a cauldron.

She led him to a rolling country he recognized as being north and east of Hunter's Spring. From the little pebbled ribs of barren country where winter winds scoured, he could look down and see what little of the country he had reason to remember.

"Have you ever been up here, Mister Hawk?"

"No'm, never have. It's pretty, though."

She pointed into the glazed distance where dark drops were cattle, like blood on a rumpled tapestry of tan. "The largest ranches are back in there. See that place against the foothills? That's Franklin Bosworth's ranch. The one closer in is Ned Smith's TJ outfit."

"You must be a native."

"I am."

Their eyes held briefly, then she was telling him of the country as they rode, pointing it out until they reined up among fragrant trees in a shady stand, with needles oil-spongy underfoot, and a chuckling little spring making a fern-like coolness. The water was so translucent every pebble was a separate world beneath it.

He let his horse edge in and drink, making noises as the water and air flowed upward against the cricket in the bit.

"Once there was an outlaw came right here," she said, "and my father's told me how the Mexicans used to come up here with goat-bladder water bags and fill them."

He got down, and loosened his horse's cinch. She dismounted, too, and did a better job of watering her horse because she slipped the bridle off, using the snugged-up reins to hold him by. "Is this land rough enough?" she asked, seeing the way his head was turned, thoughtful gaze skimming the distance toward Hunter's Spring, barely visible in the heat haze.

"Yes, I think so."

"Have we gone far enough for you to tell, yet?"

He made a cigarette, lit it, and put his hat atop his saddle horn. The shade felt cool on his head, through his pressed-down hair. "I reckon so."

"Well . . . ?"

"Tell me something, Miss Porter. If a man rode toward Vacaville from back in this country . . . would he pass Hunter's Spring? I mean, is that the way most folks travel to town on horseback?"

She was studying his face when she said: "They might. I'd say if they were natives, they probably would because it's the only place to water animals before town." A shrug. "There are other trails, though."

He squatted. "I wonder how Hunter's Spring got its name."

She looked around and downward, into the dancing distance. "I don't believe I've ever heard, but it seems rather obvious, doesn't it?"

"There are more kinds of hunters than the rabbit kind," he said, and smiled.

She was standing sideways and a little breeze came along to press against her.

"This is a beautiful spot up here, Miss Porter," he said.

"But hot."

"Yes, hot," he echoed, drew inward on his cigarette, and said: "Vacaville's so quiet, it's hard to believe it has a reputation as a rough town. At least now, in the summer."

She smiled a young-old smile at him. "You don't know Vacaville, Mister Hawk. It's been fairly quiet lately, but it never stays that way. Perhaps it's the heat." She leaned upon her saddled horse. "About ten days ago there was a spectacular robbery, though."

And he'd been fishing for that nearly an hour. "Oh?" he said.

She looked northward again. "That big ranch I pointed out . . . the Bosworth place . . . had about sixty head of saddle horses stolen."

"No," he said, looking straight into the depths of her eyes, not the least bit shocked.

"Yes, someone rode into their holding pasture, cut out the best animals, and drove them off."

He blinked. "Out of their pasture?"

"Yes, and the track was as plain as day to Hunter's Spring. After that the thieves split up. One went south toward Mexico while the other one took the horses west. As far as I've heard, he hasn't been caught yet."

He rolled a bewildered—"Well!"—off his tongue and kept right on looking at her. Until she smiled at him.

"So you see, perhaps the heat may keep a few outlaws quiet, but it doesn't appear to depress all of them."

"No," he said, gazing with vast interest into the burning tip of his cigarette.

"And they all had Bosworth's Pothook brand on them, which is well known."

John stumped out the cigarette, leaned upon the spongy earth, pushed, and stood upright. "Out of the pasture," he said. "Odd, didn't anyone hear them?"

"Mister Bosworth told my father no one heard a sound.

Didn't even know the horses were gone until the next morning."

"This is very strange."

She nodded at him. "They intended to use the horses the very next day, for roundup."

"Oh." He was looking past her head in an absorbed way. "The thief may have known the horses had been gathered, put in that pasture. He may even have known Bosworth's riders would be using them the next day."

"They knew more than that," she said. "They knew which were the best horses, too. Only sixty were taken of eighty or so."

"I see," John said, and sat down again, and perception came. The two men in the café—the cowboy he'd given his $100 to—were horse thieves. And he'd stolen someone named Bosworth's horses from the men who'd originally stolen them.

She said: "It's so quiet up here, I love it."

"Yes, isn't it?"

"To get back to my horse. . . ."

"Excuse me, I want a drink."

He got it, kneeling, supping up the cold water, and later sitting back, scooping up handfuls of it to hold against his face, letting it spill against his shirt front. Trickled some into his hair where it was even cooler.

Back beside her on the soft-scented earth he said: "Your horse doesn't seem to have a hoof felon after all."

She was hugging her drawn-up knees, looking southward. In a liquid and relieved way she said: "I'm so glad."

He leaned back, tucked a pine needle between his teeth, and gazed at the molten landscape running southward so that it appeared to be bisecting thin shadows that were coming from beneath rocks, out of the flesh of trees, over the lips of depressions.

"Tell me, Miss Porter, does Vacaville have a lot of successful

23

people in it?"

Her gaze curved around and downward, puzzled-looking. "How do you mean . . . successful?"

"Oh, I reckon like bankers, liverymen, merchants . . . gamblers, too, maybe. You know, successful men." Because the man at the cafe had been well-dressed, successful-looking, although his companion had appeared to be a common rider.

"I suppose Vacaville has its share," she mused.

"There's one in particular," he said, "but I can't recollect his name."

"Oh. Mister Courtland? He's the banker."

"No, that's not it?"

"Jameson? He owns the livery barn. Sargent? He owns the largest mercantile."

"They don't sound right, either."

"Houghton? Murphy, Groggins, Perkins, Smalley, Stevenson . . . ?"

"Smalley might be right. Who is he?"

"Jeff Smalley. He owns the Running Horse Saloon."

"Running Horse. . . . Nice name."

She looked disapproving but he didn't see it. "It's not a nice place."

"Oh, excuse me." He looked up, but she was profiled, looking into the land of lengthening shadows.

"It's where a lot of the miners and freighters and common riders go. Mister Smalley used to be town marshal years ago. He has a large trade, which is obvious because you can hear the racket from the Running Horse almost any night."

The resin-tainted pine needle in his mouth tasted bitter. He spat it out. "Maybe that's not the right man," he said. "I don't recollect that the man I was thinking of ran a saloon. It doesn't matter anyway. I just thought that a stranger in town ought to know someone."

She gazed down at him. "But you have Mister O'Brien."

He blinked again. "Yes, of course. I've got him, haven't I?"

And they both laughed but with different reasons and she jumped up. "We'd better go back. It'll be dusk by the time I get home."

He took his hat from the saddle horn and turned it in his fingers like it wasn't visible; he had to feel it to be sure what it was. She mounted gracefully and looked down at him.

"Miss Porter, would you show me some more of your country, sometime?"

"I imagine so, Mister Hawk," she said, and they rode back through the descending coolness with the tangy scent of desert around them.

CHAPTER TWO

He walked in the softness of dusk, listening to the cadence of footfalls against the plank walk. He had the money, $600 of it. More money than he'd ever had before at one time. He'd made his first step upward and the beautiful girl had smiled at him. And overhead the moon was like a Mexican dagger, curved and sharp-edged. The stars appeared foreign, though, unlike other stars he'd slept beneath. Strangers that shone with disapproval in their coldness and the big bowl of heaven was blindly dark, smothering, so he walked, looking at the scuffed planks underfoot until the walkway petered out, merged with ageless dust.

He walked past shacks with sunken-eyed windows, black and cavernous. Thought of Joyce and worry, anxiety, walked with him, for all he was hoping for depended upon an unknown horse thief in Mexico. Joyce and a springy-walking, lean man with a pinched-up face. They were unknowingly life and death, defeat or victory, success or failure. And he saw the future with stark lucidity. It was clear-cut and smelled of death and hang ropes, which frightened him, because sooner or later time must run out for him, one way or another.

He walked through the muffling dust of a crooked footpath as far as a scraggly oak and leaned against it, looking back toward town. He saw the winking orange lights, warm and friendly, that he was shut away from in a quandary of loneliness. Sweat squeezed out of his pores cold with isolation.

26

Persisting in what he'd envisioned, he had to employ the $600 to make $1,200, $12,000, as much as he could. And if he failed, what? Simple enough, he thought. Steal more horses. Better yet, rob a bullion stage or a bank. Get thousands instead of hundreds. And that was the future that he saw so vividly, and knew. That was how men became outlaws. Through failure. By repeating their initial outlawry. Sequences flowed through his mind, and the path upward to respectability became more difficult to attain with each step back, behind a gun. The trail back was patched a mile with bodies and lives.

Perspiration upon his forehead showed transparently in the moonlight. He'd taken the long odds and the risk still hung over him. He'd never do it again, so the $600 had to succeed for him. He'd have to *make* it succeed the first time. Urgency stayed in him, the walk of a girl dimmed while his mind closed down around the next phase of existence. Ambition of a calculating kind began to obsess him.

He stomped out the cigarette and trudged back to town, thoughts moving ponderously behind his face, and just before he entered the Running Horse Saloon he looked upward at the forbidding sky. It was warm, stars wiggling their old raffish encouragement, fellow conspirators a million miles away. Confidence swept through him.

He moved twistingly through the noise and smell of the Running Horse and almost immediately saw Jeff Smalley, whose solid figure fascinated him, wedded to dread. He recognized Smalley's bitter slit of a mouth, the detached way he leaned listening to another man's talk.

John bought a glass of ale and went to a corner with it, and watched the crowd and thought of Smalley, for he surely knew by now that the rustled horses had been stolen from him. He surmised that an unspeakable, choking fury possessed the man. He dared say nothing. That silently outraged, gagged kind of

anger was the deadliest kind. It burned unappeased and unap-
peasable, incapable of expression, living within a man always,
swollen, stifled.

He stood in the echoing corner seeing faces, identifying them,
relating them to situations, places, like the irritable farrier's face
and the cigar-sucking liveryman's face, and when he was satisfied with the pulse of the saloon, he left. He went down the
road to the Eagle Hotel, arranged for a room, and slept in a
bed.

The following morning he was finishing breakfast in the
restaurant he'd first patronized in Vacaville when the shrill call
of the dawn stage rolled musically high and still through the
quietude. He made a cigarette and went outside to watch the
coach and four swirl up from the south with a flourish, bend
toward the plank walk before the stage office, and settle back
upon leather springs with a proud lurch.

A boy with a running nose and horse safety pins holding
ragged clothing together went awkwardly to each wheel with a
lard bucket of grease. He snuffled and greased while the driver
furled his silver-ferruled whip, badge of an arrogant profession,
swooped a gloved hand beneath a longhorn mustache, winked
grandly at the clerk on the walkway, and began to climb down.
The gun guard got down more stiffly, face drawn and gray-
appearing, mouth fallen in against toothless gums, his carbine
worn and battered-looking.

The passengers alighted, three men in suits, bowlers, and one
cowboy munching a red apple, looking at Vacaville like one stray
eyes another stray.

The old guard stumped around the rear of the coach, up to
the clerk with the baby face, and held out the carbine. "All
yours," he said, "and you know what you can do with it."

The clerk didn't take the gun. He looked at the guard with
an embarrassed expression, fingers tightening upon the clip

board he held. "Now, Arch," he said. "Let's wait until tonight."

"Not tonight or any other night," the guard said, and leaned the company gun against a rear wheel and walked away.

From across the road John watched it all, the panorama of a stage arriving, the minute drama of each moment. Hostlers were unharnessing the teams, leading them away. The little knot of men broke, scattered. The coach was left to stand empty, forlorn and earth-bound, its romantic sparkle departing with the horses.

The cowboy took up a saddle, balanced it upon a hip, and began walking stiltedly northward toward the livery barn, munching his apple, and except for his height he might have been ten years old.

John stood motionlessly until the sun touched his right side, then crossed the roadway to the stage office. The clerk was putting on sleeve protectors of black alpaca. He looked up and nodded. A gentle, diffident face set above a mild chin.

"Can I help you?"

John bent from the waist, leaning upon the counter. "Did your guard quit?" he asked.

The soft eyes became embarrassed again, and dropped. "I think so," the clerk said softly. "He's quit before, though." It lay between them indecisively.

"Well, that's too bad. Is the owner around?"

"No. He owns the livery barn. Most of the time he's down there."

"I see. What's his name?"

"Mister Jameson."

"Thanks." John started to turn.

"Uh . . . would you be interested in the job?"

"I might," John said.

"Well, I believe you can get it. Mister Jameson's a little short of patience. It's possible he won't take old Arch back this time."

"I'll go see him. Thanks again."

He returned to the roadway where the full light was falling with its summer dryness. He went down to the livery barn and found the swamper, who looked up at him from behind the bristly broom.

"Mister Jameson around?"

"Not yet," the swamper said. "Say, don't you own that big bay horse? Well, I washed him down and grained him yesterday, you recall."

John dug out coins and held them out wordlessly. At the sound of heavy footsteps he turned. The liveryman was looking at him with a false geniality.

"Mister Jameson?"

"Yes, sir. How can I serve you?"

"I understand you need a new gun guard on your coach line."

"Oh," Jameson said, still moving. "Come into the office."

Brittle dust and ledgers, sweat scent, stale cigar smoke overlay the small room. Jameson fell into a bucket chair still wearing his humorless smile. "Did Arch quit again?" he asked.

"Yes."

"In that case," Jameson said, "I expect I do need another guard, don't I?" The eyes became measuring, weighing in their withdrawn way. "Are you qualified?"

"I've ridden as gun guard before," John said. Then, without knowing exactly why, he added: "Actually what I'm looking for is something to invest in around Vacaville."

"Is that so?" Jameson's regard became sharper. "Want a job until you get the feel of the country, is that it?"

"Yes."

"I see. Well, that makes sense. What's your name?"

"John Hawk."

"All right, John, you're hired. I'll give you a note to my clerk. He'll give you the schedules." Jameson bent, writing, and words flowed upward from him. "The runs are safe enough but mail contracts specify that common carriers must employ gun guards." He got up heavily, held out the note in one hand, and extended his other hand. John pumped the free hand and dropped it, took the note, and left the office. The memory of Jameson's insincerity lingered.

At the stage office the clerk took the note without speaking. Studied it in his diffident way and said: "I'll make up a schedule for you, Mister Hawk. If you'll come back a little later. . . ."

"Call me John. Fine, I'll be back later on. Thanks."

The clerk's embarrassment was acute when he took the big hand and shook it, eyes averted. "My name's Cleve," he said, and was relieved when John left, walked out into the roadway, and saw Joyce Porter approaching.

He waited until she was close. " 'Morning, ma'am," he said.

"Good morning, Mister Hawk. Aren't the mornings wonderful?"

"They sure are. Care if I walk with you?"

She smiled through a little nod, and they went south, making conversation that never ventured beyond a résumé of things they had done and discussed at their last meeting, until he told her he'd been hired as gun guard by Jameson. She slowed without speaking and finally stopped under the overhang before Murphy's Emporium for general goods and hardware.

"You must like Vacaville," she said.

"Yes, I like it."

"I'm glad. It's a nice town in spite of some of the things that happen in it." She smiled again, turned to enter the store, and in a demure way said: "Mister O'Brien said he thought you'd stay."

And she disappeared inside.

He knew people were stepping around him but he didn't move for a moment, then he walked toward the livery barn, cut

31

around in back, and found the irascible farrier smoking a cigar and scowling moodily at a tied horse.

"Good morning."

"Hunh."

He leaned upon an upright post watching the acid face, waiting. In his own good time the farrier turned to look at him. There was a squinted look to his face. Without preliminary he said: "So I sent you over to look at a horse, did I?"

"I didn't say that. I said you'd hinted that I might look at her horse."

"A lie is a lie," O'Brien said growlingly. "And what's more I don't need the likes of you to look at horses for me."

"No," John said, "I don't expect you do."

"And I know why you did that, too."

"You probably do. What I'm curious about is what you told her."

"Told her nothing," O'Brien said. "Her or nobody else. If you want to make a horse's rear-end out of yourself to meet a girl, it's none of my business." He turned his back and resumed the interrupted study of the tied horse. Cigar smoke erupted in short, upward gusts.

John said—"Thanks."—and walked away.

O'Brien turned when the footsteps were dying and gazed after the soft-walking big man. His face showed nothing of his thoughts.

At the stage office Curt Jameson was pressing his meek clerk down with heavy words. Cleve's face was pale, weak mouth loose, gently suffering-looking. At John's entrance Jameson turned. The mechanical smile came up. "Cleve has your schedule," he said, flagged with a broad hand, and left.

The air in the office was depressing. John accepted the proffered paper from Cleve without looking at it. "What kind of a man is Jameson, anyway?" he asked.

Cleve's eyes swung up, then sideways and down again. In a subdued voice he said: "He's a good businessman."

John studied the schedule with slightly knitted brows and Cleve rattled papers upon his desk as though there might be something lurking beneath them. When John sighed, Cleve looked up quickly.

"Can you make it out?"

John slouched upon the counter. "Yeah, it's clear enough. I go out at six this evening, bunk down at Springerville, and ride the dawn coach back tomorrow."

"Yes."

John folded the paper and put it in a shirt pocket, nodded at Cleve, and went outside.

The heat was flat and encompassing, like the sunlight it was made of. No shade. Even the scruffy dogs nosing along the edge of the roadway cast no shadows. Across the road and down a ways several men stood under an overhang, talking. One was Jeff Smalley, recognizable by his stockiness, his clothing, and the cant of his head. The others appeared to be townsmen of some kind, perhaps gamblers.

Then began the long flow of days, golden, blurred by sameness. To John they had familiarity of a kind, a blend of heat and the fierce light of the land. He came to know people, stage drivers, hostlers, passengers. Knowledge of the terrain southward came, too, and eventually gossip lent a feeling of permanency to him, as though he had known Vacaville and its inhabitants a lifetime.

Days of riding beside a longhorn-mustached driver named Ford Tull, a vain, dashing man, grand of gesture, flashing of eye, prototype of his calling and peacock-proud of it. Days that telescoped themselves became weeks, and eventually the occupational disease of gun guards in a safe, organized community, set in—boredom. A time for restless thoughts to persist in their annoyances.

For John these were especially troublous because his feeling of urgency had never lessened. The knowledge that was locked inside his mind, the fear and certainty of eventual disclosure, the sense that time was hurrying while he was only marking it. Much to do but he was doing nothing, was reverting to the ways of a drifter. Letting the fresh days spin past while he rocked atop a Springerville-Vacaville stage, squinting into distances that were hot and moving.

Then, in the third week of September, his schedule was altered and he rode the evening stage southward instead of the daylight stage. It was the breaking of habit, apparently nothing more. There was no explanation, just a note from Cleve signed by Jameson making the shift, and he rocked with the coach, listening to Ford Tull's scratchy song. Watching hypnotic rumps of big horses rise and fall, rise and fall.

Until the road bent, lazy-like, a tired old snake all mottled with shade and dull pebbles, jackknifing back to meet itself at a switchback.

And the first inkling he had of trouble was a whistling snort from the off leader. The startled way the animal threw up its head and changed leads, slowing. Then he saw the masked man and the solitary black eye as big as all outdoors, of a shotgun thrust upward.

"Haul up!"

Ford pulled and braced against the foot brake, erupted wordless breath behind his elegant mustache, and kept both hands high. Dusk was settling implacably, making the wispy shadow with the shotgun something unreal, elusive, and lean to the eye.

"Guard, throw down that gun!"

John let the carbine fall out and down. He tried to limn the man but his eyes refused to leave the big bore that pointed steadily up at him. The man remained vague.

"Now your handguns."

They were also thrown down. Then the highwayman left the protection of the big horse's body and walked springily back. From off to one side he said: "No passengers, eh? That's good." A wispy laugh, dry-hard with keyed-up nerves, sounded. "Got to be cagey," the robber said, mostly to himself. And John's heart stood perfectly still.

That voice, those springy movements, the wispiness of the man. . . . He bent outward a little, peering down. And the lean size. . . .

"Is the box in the boot?"

Ford spoke very clearly. "It's up here, yes."

"Then throw it down. And watch it, fellers," the masked face said. "Let's get along."

Without moving, Ford Tull said: "Throw it down, guard." His hands were still high, rigid with lines flowing downward from them.

John moved off the seat, balanced himself in the boot, bent, and grasped their payload. It was heavy enough to make him strain and he knew why the schedule had been altered. He turned in the cramped space and looked down at the shadowy highwayman. A silhouette blended with the evening, nothing distinguishable except the shotgun.

"Throw it. If it busts, so much the better."

John threw it and before it struck the blue-black glitter of that long barrel was waving at them.

"Drive on, fellers, and don't be foolish. Just keep on going."

Ford Tull lowered his arms with a creak in the shoulders and flipped the lines. The horses leaned, the coach rattled, and night was down solidly as they pulled away. They went half a mile before the motionless, silent guard reached over, grasped the lines and drew backward. Tull's face was a pale blur with a dividing line between upper and lower features. He set the foot brake. The stage came to a gradual halt.

"What for?" Tull said.

"I'm going back. He won't take that box far. It was too heavy."

"Don't be a damned fool. He's armed to the teeth."

John was descending via the fore wheel. "When you get back, round up a posse and bring an extra horse for me."

Ford Tull protested until John was on the ground, where he turned northward and disappeared. Tull loosened his hold on the lines, kicked at the brake, and the coach moved off.

Darkness was an ally until John got back where the coach had been waylaid, then it became an enemy. He had to walk bent over to make out any tracks at all and at best they were very faint.

He was impatient with a moon that took so long to come up and by the time there was watery light to aid him he thought the highwayman was either miles away or deadly close.

Shod horse tracks upon the filmy dust made occasional smooth tracks that caught and faintly reflected their passage. It was these tantalizingly spaced smudges that kept John going in the right direction. But twice in one hour he lost his way, and when thirst began to annoy him, he felt lost in an immensity of gloomy silence both limitless and unfriendly.

Desperation of a purely private sort kept him going. He knew who the highwayman was; it was vital that he find him before Ford Tull got back to Vacaville, roused up a posse, and returned. Urgency crawled out along his nerves when the trail grew maddeningly faint and dead grass began to obliterate it altogether. When he finally ran out of sign altogether, stopped, straightened up, and swore, the world lay prone and stilled, unconcerned, unwilling to take or yield impressions.

But the urgency started him moving, walking, trying to cope with the darkness, and when fate intervened, it wasn't the ground or the night that opened up and let him through, it was

36

sound. Somewhere ahead a gun was fired against a shuddering object, close and booming, throwing throttled resonance upward and outward in a choked way.

John began to trot toward the echoes with them whispering past and around him. Trotting and hoping he might get close before the highwayman scooped up the sacks of coin and rode on, lighter and hurrying.

He first saw the dimmest outline of a horse against the skyline. Next he saw the moving figure, wispy and lean. The thing that stopped him, brought him low, was a sheen of gun metal. From a pressed flat position he called to the highwayman.

"You're covered! Don't move!"

The bent figure froze motionlessly but the dull glow of gun metal slewed around, grew probing and full of menace.

"Listen," John said quickly. "I'm not here to arrest you or take that money, so stand up straight and keep your gun pointing down."

But the hunched figure didn't straighten up. After a while the highwayman said: "Who are you?"

"Do like I said!"

Slowly the gunman straightened, lowered his gun, and with defiance in his voice said: "All right, mister, it's your deal."

And John arose, went forward with his empty hip holster slapping against his thigh. When he was close enough for the outlaw to see him, the gun barrel tilted upward into lethal alignment and stayed there. Small eyes grated in their sockets when John stopped.

"Put up the gun," he said. "I'm unarmed."

"So I see," the highwayman said without holstering his gun. "You were the guard, weren't you? I recognize that hat."

"Is that all you recognize?" John asked.

It was dark and John was twenty feet away. The outlaw

shrugged. "Yeah. Come up closer."

The outlaw cocked his head when John moved in, then moved a little and said: "Hell's bells."

"You know me now?"

"Sure. You're the feller took delivery on the horses for Jeff Smalley. What in hell are you doing riding gun guard on a coach?"

"Killing time," John said.

The outlaw relaxed a little and perplexity showed in his face. "Well," he said waspishly, "I don't understand, but then I reckon it's none of my business what you do anyway." He motioned toward the shattered box with his gun barrel. "Now what?" he asked.

John ignored the box, the pouches lying beside it. "Were you on your way to Vacaville?"

"Yeah, going back to get some money from Jeff."

"How did you know the stage had bullion on it?"

"I didn't. Every now and then life gives a feller a nice surprise. This was mine." The little eyes grew ironic. "But you sure pulled a dumb stunt shagging me like that. If I'd seen you first. . . ."

"You didn't. What's your name?"

"Jack Keeney'll do. What's yours?"

"John Hawk."

And the highwayman's teeth shone thinly. "That'll do, too," he said.

"Jack, take that money and keep on going. Forget Vacaville."

The outlaw wagged his head. "Nope. I've got money coming from Smalley. I aim to get it."

"You'll get hung sure as shooting."

"For robbing the stage? I don't think so. You're the only one'd recognize me, John Hawk."

"Don't sell Smalley short. The stage's held up, you arrive in town afterward."

"To hell with Smalley. Say, just what's all this leading to?"

"I don't want you in town," John said.

The highwayman's still eyes grew puzzled, thin eyebrows descended, formed a straight line across the lean face. "I don't savvy," he said. "And what difference does it make to me what you want, anyway?"

"I'll tell you. Those horses you rustled from that big ranch northeast of town. . . ."

"What about them?"

"You delivered them to me."

"What of it?"

"I wasn't sent after them by Smalley."

The outlaw's puzzlement deepened. He stood loosely, gun hanging, mouth tucked inward.

"I knew Smalley was to give you a hundred-dollar advance for them. I took a chance you'd think I was Smalley's man, met you, gave you the hundred, and took the horses."

"Well, I'll be damned. You mean you stole the horses from me?"

"No, I stole them from Smalley. What I didn't know was that they were stolen horses in the first place."

"Wait a minute, Hawk," the highwayman said. "You stole them from me because Smalley was to peddle them and I was to get half the money from their sale." Astonishment glazed the outlaw's eyes, loosened the muscles of his pinched-up face. "I'll be gone to hell," he said. "It's got so's you can't trust *anybody*. This is the damnedest piece of work I ever heard of."

John said: "You're the only person who can identify me as the man who took the horses from you . . . now do you understand?"

But the highwayman's thoughts were elsewhere. He said: "I'll bet Smalley's ripe to busting."

John drove ahead with his own thoughts. "And I'm the only one that can identify you as the stage robber."

The outlaw fell silent, remained that way for a long time, then his expression cleared. "I see," he said. "You want to trade. I keep my mouth shut and you'll keep yours shut. That it?"

"That's it."

"You don't have much trading stock, John Hawk. Hell, I can leave you here by the bullion box"—he wiggled the gun suggestively—"and still go see Smalley."

"But you won't get any money from him," John said. "I sold the horses. He didn't."

"Yeah, that's right, isn't it? And you'll pay me for the horses. Right?"

"No, not exactly, but I'll forget who you are. You got enough money off the stage tonight, anyway. All I'm asking is that you forget my face so I can forget yours."

The highwayman said: "John, this calls for some figuring. I never run into anything like this before." He lapsed into silence.

"You haven't got that much time," John said. "The coach went back to Vacaville. There's a posse riding right now."

The highwayman cocked his head in a listening posture for a second.

"As gun guard on the Vacaville-Springerville stage, you can find me around the stage office almost any time. While you're thinking this over, all I ask is that you don't tell Smalley who I am. Just say you'd recognize the horse thief but haven't seen him since . . . anything you want to say so long as you don't point me out."

"Doesn't he even suspect you?"

"No, of course not. You're the only person who saw me."

"Hmmm, I reckon that could be right, at that."

"It *is* right. If it wasn't . . . if he suspected who I was . . . would I be riding around like I'm doing, under his nose?"

"No."

"Then he doesn't know. Nobody but you knows."

"Damnedest thing I ever heard of," the highwayman said. "What did you do with those horses, anyway?"

"I told you. I sold them just like Smalley was going to do."

Another silence, then the outlaw slowly holstered his gun and scratched himself. "Smalley'll be spitting bullets by now," he said absently.

"Is it a trade?" John's mind was ticking off time. "If we stand around here much longer, you'll get shot or hung, I can promise you that."

And the highwayman cocked his head again, shuffled his feet, and gazed long at the bullion sacks beside the shattered box. "I got to get used to this," he said, then looked up into John's face and rested his hands on his hips.

"You know where I'll be."

"Do I? What's to keep you from lighting out?"

John snorted. "After I sold those horses and came back here proves I've got reasons for staying around, doesn't it?"

"Or you're crazy," the outlaw said.

"All right," John said impatiently. "Crazy or not, I'm here, and, if you'll keep your mouth shut, I'm going to stay."

"I guess," the outlaw said slowly, "there's no sense in my asking what all this is about, is there?"

"No."

Then the bandit drew himself up to his full height. "All right, John Hawk, you got a temporary trade. I'll take the bullion and keep quiet about who you are . . . you do likewise, but if you got some scheme in the back of your head and cross me up, I can give you a pretty good idea of what Smalley'll do when he finds out who you are. Understand?"

"I understand, and I've got better reasons to be quiet than you have."

41

"I hope you have."

The highwayman turned away, went to his horse, lashed down the off-side saddlebag flap, returned for the rest of the little bullion sacks, threw them into the near-side bag, mounted, and gazed downward at the motionless figure near the broken box.

"Stall them off, John," he said companionably. "They won't be able to read my sign before sunup anyway. See you in Vacaville." And he loped out into the darkness.

John remained where he was with tangents running random-like through his mind, each thought ending against a question that held back a deluge of danger. He stood, wide-legged and alone, before the truth that could destroy him, and thought of the solidity of his personal position—which of course wasn't solid at all.

He was sitting by the broken box when the posse came. There was no point in lying to them for dawn wasn't far off, so he simply said he'd arrived by the box after the outlaw had gone on, then suggested they all waited until dawn, which they did. By then the trail was clear enough but the highwayman was long gone.

Curt Jameson was among those who stood foremost among the crowd that welcomed the posse back just before noon. His cigar was upthrust and unlit, small eyes without any of their customary false amiability.

The posse dismounted stiffly and questions washed up and over them. A few of the riders ignored them, led their horses away without speaking. Some were profanely disgusted at their lack of success while John was totally silent until Cleve reached over and touched his sleeve.

"No luck?" he said, and blushed furiously.

John handed him the reins to his horse without answering and headed for a water trough. He drank until his belly felt tight, then rinsed his face and plunged his shirted arms deep into the water. A shimmering reflection of something white moved across the ripples he set up. He ignored it.

Sweat burst out and ran in funnels under his shirt. He leaned upon the trough, looking back where the crowd lingered. Curled up a cigarette, lit it, and exhaled dry-hot smoke.

Down the road by the Running Horse Saloon a knot of men stood idly, watching the posse disband. He saw Jeff Smalley among them. The man's stance symbolized boredom and that was all.

John exhaled a mighty lungful of blue smoke.

"You look tired."

He turned and saw her smile. "Yes'm, I am."

"Did you find anything?"

"The posse didn't, no."

"That's too bad. Everyone in town is speculating on who he was."

"Would anyone be likely to know?" he asked.

"They probably would," she said, "if there was anything to go on. Bullion stages aren't common."

And John's voice sounded dull. "Maybe he was just lucky in that respect," he said.

"Maybe."

She stood in the shade, looking a thousand desirable miles away to him. Cool and beautiful and unruffled. There was neither anxiety nor urgency to her.

The sun drove down hard against him and he knew he'd drunk too much water because it was backing up with green bile into his throat. "Excuse me," he said, and walked away.

CHAPTER THREE

Curt Jameson made it a point to be on hand the following evening when John's coach returned from Springerville. He looked aggressively mean and intolerant. John caught his head motion and went deep into the stage office, following, trailing the company .30 carbine. Jameson came around near the back wall where shadows nested.

"Haven't had much chance to talk to you about that robbery," he said. "What are your ideas about it?"

John leaned on the short gun, had to bend a little to do it. In Jameson's face was reflected his inner self. The calculating, secretly despising man he really was. As cold as winter, as bleak and untrustworthy, as shrewd and dangerous as a rattler. John saw it, recognized it, filed the impressions away. "What kind of ideas?" he asked.

"About the robber. You saw him. What was he like?"

"Oh, medium size, I'd say. Medium build. Nothing outstanding about him."

Jameson made a dissatisfied grunt. "That's no help."

"No," John replied, "and neither was the night."

Jameson seemed torn between a desire to be mean, and not to be. He rummaged with both hands in his various pockets and finally dredged up a cigar, plunged it into his mouth, and bit down on it, hard.

"That robbery cost the stage company seven thousand dollars. What do you think of that?"

John watched the heavy, vicious face and left his dislike deep down. "What should I think about it?" he said. "I did all one man could do, you know. Let Vacaville law take it from there."

"Vacaville law," Jameson snorted. "As soon turn loose a bunch of kids. Deputies had any brains they wouldn't be underpaid damned fools, they'd be businessmen."

And John continued to lean on the carbine, studying the coarse face, repelled but saying nothing.

Jameson deplored the robbery in flat tones and finally cast out the core of his wrath and said: "John, it amounts to this as far as I'm concerned. I can't run both businesses. By God, they'll rob me blind because I'm not twins. Now then, for five thousand I'll sell you half the stage company. You'll run it and we'll split. Half of everything, horses, coaches, harness, buildings, sheds, everything. For five thousand."

But John straightened up off the carbine and looked past Jameson at the wall, because $600 gained at risk of death was so pitifully small, so inadequate. "I might make some kind of a deal," he said slowly, "if I had five thousand dollars, but I haven't. Nowhere near that much money."

"But you wouldn't have to pay it all now," Jameson said. "Just a fifth of it now. A thousand, say."

"Five hundred?"

Jameson's neck swelled. "Five hundred? Why, man, any of the teams'd fetch more'n that. That isn't even. . . ."

"Five hundred's about it, Mister Jameson," John said. "I could make it six but that's all."

"Six hundred dollars," Jameson said hollowly. "You're trying to make me mad, John."

John smiled at him, enjoying it. "Well," he said, "I want to get over to the barbershop and get a bath before he closes."

"Wait a second, John. Dammit all, man, you can do better'n a lousy six hundred dollars."

"No, I can't. Six hundred and the rest to come out of the profits."

"At eight percent on the unpaid balance."

"No, four percent, Mister Jameson. For all I know that'll take half a lifetime."

And Curt Jameson, in a very matter-of-fact way, said: "Well, damn! All right then, but I hope your conscience bothers you tonight. Meet me at the livery barn in the morning. We'll go to the lawyer's and draw up partnership papers. Six hundred down, the balance in prorated monthly installments out of profits at four percent."

"Can't in the morning. I'll be leaving on the southbound coach."

But Jameson waved a hand. "Get a substitute," he said, and stomped past, toward the doorway and the plank walk beyond.

John put up the gun and sauntered as far as Cleve's desk behind the counter. He curved a pensive stare at the clerk's hunched-over form.

"Cleve, is the company making money?"

Cleve looked up, surprised, his color mounting, eyes liquidly soft, shy-looking. "Well, yes, the line makes money. Maybe with a few changes it might make a little more, but I don't know. . . ."

"Don't know what?"

Cleve became confused, diffident. His hands fluttered, soft-white, vague, flustered. "Oh, little things, John," he said, and his eyes begged John not to drive him.

"You mean like tighter schedules, better stock, maybe. Things like that?"

"Those things," Cleve said, and turned away quickly. "But it isn't for us to say, you know," he went on almost gently. "It's Mister Jameson's concern, not ours."

"Maybe. Maybe not. I'm going to buy half interest from him, you see."

Cleve's face drained, his shyness became something else, shock, astonishment, a variety of fear that lurks in every natural coward and jumps out at sight of any change. "You are?" he said.

"Yes."

John turned away from the weak face and walked slowly out of the office. Walked with his thoughts. Put each foot down ahead of its mate, thinking he was building something substantial upon a foundation of sand—and hang ropes.

He went to the café and ate mechanically, paid for a meal he didn't remember, and walked until the shadows began to creep out in his wake and trudge along paths older than anything.

"Mister Hawk."

He drew up and peered from under his hat brim at her, and a peculiar boldness gripped him. He bowed a little. "Miss Porter." Their glances held and he said: "I wonder if you'd do me a favor, ma'am."

"Probably," she said, half smiling, waiting.

"Walk with me to the north end of town and back again."

She looked a little surprised, then laughed at him. "At suppertime? I have a father to feed."

"Oh," he said, and looked past her.

She watched him a moment, then said: "Why don't you come and eat with us, instead."

"I just finished supper, thanks just the same." He was starting past her.

"Wait," she said. "If you'll come by the house in an hour, I'd love to go for a walk."

So he nodded at her. "In an hour then, ma'am." And he passed on with his thoughts growing heavier as he trudged, weighing him down with strangeness that was partly dread of the future and partly a fierce kind of exhilaration that dared him to make good with the stage line, risk or no risk.

By the time he was back at her house, she was a pale silhouette on the porch that descended the steps like a wraith and sailed toward him, eyes large and dark-looking, full of mystery and night. She hesitated inside the gate, watching him. A strange man, large, gentle-looking, but tantalizingly strange in some indefinable way.

They walked northward.

"Do they know anything more about the robbery?" she asked.

"Not that I know of," he told her. "Mister Jameson said it cost the line seven thousand dollars."

"I heard that," she said. "It was an especially chartered stage to the Springerville bank with Franklin Bosworth's money."

He looked around and down. "Bosworth? The same man who lost the horses?"

"Yes. Doesn't it seem that trouble comes like that, sometimes, all at one time?"

He made a short laugh. "All at one time, yes."

From beneath her lashes she looked up at him, watched a splash of orange lamplight cut across his face from a window they were passing, then the darkness returned, and she said: "How is Mister O'Brien?"

They were near a little church with a thin cross askew atop it. He looked down at the plank steps and motioned toward them. "Could we sit here, do you reckon?"

"I'm sure we could." And she sat down, drew her legs up, and clasped arms around them.

He sat heavily, lay back, and pushed his legs out, crossed them at the ankles, and regarded his boot toes solemnly. "Mister O'Brien, ma'am, is no particular friend of mine."

She smiled at the night, head up a little. "He's not too well liked, I know."

"I didn't mean that. I meant I don't know him, not really."

"No?" she said with soft inflection, still looking at the darkness.

"No. And I don't want to have that lie between us, you see. I saw you the day you took your lame horse to his shop. Then, the day I came over and told you I'd like to look at the horse . . . well, O'Brien didn't send me at all."

She turned a little. "I know that, Mister Hawk," she said.

"You do?"

"Yes, it was rather obvious."

After a moment of looking at each other, they both began to laugh, she with humor, he with self-conscious embarrassment, chagrin. Then he listened to the night, to the song stars sing to one another. Heard the sighing breath of darkness. All in his mind.

"Did you know, when we rode up in back of town?"

"Not then. I began to suspect then, however. But after I talked with Mister O'Brien. . . ."

"I guess he wasn't hard to get the facts from, was he?"

"He wouldn't tell anyone what he didn't want to tell them. It wasn't what he said, it was the surprise he showed."

"I see," John said, and looked at her, coming to a slow respect. "Is that what folks call womankind's intuition?"

"Just a woman's suspicion, is all. But I didn't mind. You were lonely-looking. Unhappy. And you weren't forward at all."

It seemed to him they were discussing someone else, someone they both knew who was absent, and the feeling made him feel guilty. Guilt, of course, brought up other thoughts, far less pleasant. He was still for a while and she turned, gazed at him a moment, then resumed her appraisal of the night.

"Mister Hawk, why is it that trouble seems to gravitate to some people more than others?"

"Why, I expect because they go out looking for it."

"Do you?"

"Me?" He looked up. The wet light of a fat scimitar moon showed her profile like a cameo. "I haven't . . . up to now."

"Up to now?" She leaned forward a little, not looking at him. "Trouble?"

"It could be. You see, I'm the man who stole those Bosworth horses."

She was frozen, fully sculpted of pale stone. Then she twisted on the step and saw the composed, peaceful look of him. "I don't believe you, of course," she said.

"It's kind of mixed up. Another man stole them and was to deliver them to a partner, you see. Well, I heard about it and met the thief first."

"At Hunter's Spring?"

"Yes'm."

"Oh. . . ."

"Then I drove them to a town a long way off and sold them."

"Oh. . . ."

He rolled his head, looked at her, pushed himself upward, put his hat on the step beside them, and ran bent fingers through his hair.

"It could be trouble, buying into the stage company, because someone might find out about the horses. Do you see?"

"I see," she said. That, and no more.

"I reckon it was crazy to come back here."

"It was." She moved, sat a little straighter, and put both hands in her lap. She looked very prim to him. Prim and proper and he thought she was outraged, but he had no regrets, now that it was told. Just a little sad, was all.

"Why did you come back here . . . of all places?"

He was studying the back of his hand. "Just liked the place, I reckon. The place and maybe the people."

"But. . . ."

"But I'm not a horse thief. By trade, I mean. That's the first time I ever did that, and the last time."

"What possessed you . . . ?"

"I'll tell you, ma'am. I'm twenty-nine. I've ridden from Mexico to Canada. I've never been anybody and never done anything. I figured it was time I put down roots. You can't do much without money for a start."

"You could have worked and saved your money, Mister Hawk."

He smiled at her. "A rider makes maybe forty, sixty dollars a month. On a drive maybe he'll draw a hundred dollars at trail's end. A hundred dollars a couple, three times a year isn't hardly enough for a stake. But now I have a chance to buy a partnership in the Jameson stage line."

"Are you going to use the money you got from selling the horses to buy the partnership?"

"Yes'm."

"Well . . . good heavens, I'm not sure you should've told me this. You're an outlaw, you know."

"Yes'm. Once." Her voice sounded unsteady to him but her face showed nothing but a fading numbness. Shock.

She said—"Good heavens."—again, in a helpless way, and her hands fluttered briefly. Then: "Why did you tell me all this?"

"Lonely, I guess. I don't know why, exactly." He felt for his cigarette makings and bent over, hands working deftly. She watched. "It's been on my mind. Kept getting bigger and bigger. It's pretty hard for a man who's never had to make decisions . . . to start making them, ma'am."

"When you started making decisions," she said wryly, "you certainly went at it with a vengeance."

"Yes'm." He lit and exhaled, leaned back, and looked upward again. "This has been a beautiful night."

She looked swiftly at him, eyes full of meaning. "In a frightening way," she said, and fell somberly silent.

"Oh, I don't have any real regrets. What I'm trying to say is that I'm glad I told you. Told someone. Got it out in the open."

"Do you intend to tell other people, too?"

He shook his head. "No'm, I'm not that crazy. You're different."

"Mister Hawk. . . ."

"John."

". . . What do you intend to do now?"

"Work at making the stage line bigger and better. Make money like other men do."

"And the Bosworth horses?"

"I don't know exactly."

She looked away from him. The silence drew down around them, locked its grip.

"See that star up there, Miss Porter, that's the North Star. Many's the night I've talked to him on the trail."

"The night you were out with the Bosworth horses, too?"

He stirred a little and said: "No, not that night. I was too scared."

She fell silent again, absorbed with her thoughts. As remote from him as the North Star and ten times as aloof. He punched out the cigarette and took up his hat, dumped it on the back of his head, and leaned forward. "I expect we ought to go back now," he said, and there was an attitude of listening to the way he sat.

She arose, swiped at her skirt, and waited for him to unbend, stand up. "And all the time I thought other things of you."

"Like what?" he said, standing still gazing at her.

"Like you'd been disappointed in love, hurt some way back where you came from. Wronged, maybe." She started walking, faster than when she'd come down there with him. "An imagination is not always favorable to its owner, Mister Hawk."

52

After they'd walked several hundred feet he said: "But a closed mouth is, Miss Porter."

She made no reply until they came to the Porter gate. It hung ajar between them for a time and she said: "Thank you for the walk." He grinned crookedly at her. She added with meaning: "It was one I'll never forget."

She swept quickly up the walk and he turned south, trudged along the plank walk, insulated by thoughts from the noise and lights around him. Walked a little south, past the Running Horse, and someone called his name. He turned. It was Curt Jameson without his smile and a trifle flush-faced.

"Find a substitute guard yet, John?"

"I haven't looked for one."

Jameson peered. "Got to be one, you know," he said. "Our government mail contract specifies a gun guard on every coach carrying mail."

"You told me that," John said, turning away.

Jameson called after him: "See you at the barn in the morning!"

He walked through the alternate patches of lamplight and soft night with Vacaville all around him thick with man smell, vibrant with life and movement, and a dark hand from a doorway lightly touched his sleeve.

" 'Evening, John Hawk."

The pinched-up face wore its wispy smile, hard, ironic, not unfriendly.

" 'Evening, Jack," he said, cobwebs falling away, leaving his mind dagger-clear. A puckish thought came and he gazed objectively at the highwayman. "Be interested in a job?"

The outlaw's gaze was thoughtfully steady before he answered. "Might. What kind of a job?"

"Gun guard on the Springerville stage in the morning."

The highwayman laughed, little eyes puckering. "You got a

53

sense of humor," he said.

John's face remained perfectly composed, his gaze unblinking, somber. "I mean it. I can't go in the morning, and we've got to have a guard on all mail coaches. Government law."

Jack's smile thinned out. After a moment he said: "What kind of a stage line are they running anyway. First a horse thief for a guard and now a highwayman. Well, if you're serious," he added with a twinkle, "I'll do it. Just because it's funny."

John fished a stub pencil from a shirt pocket, tore the corner off a Wanted poster nailed upon the building, and wrote a note to Cleve informing him the bearer was to ride gun guard on the dawn coach. He handed it to Jack, who stepped out into better light to read it, put it carefully into a pocket with the same mocking little smile.

"I don't suppose you're doing this to get a head start on me, are you, John?"

"No."

"That's good," the outlaw said, "because I'd find you."

"I told you I'd be around."

John started to move past.

"Wait a minute," the highwayman said. "We can make a little talk here."

John turned back, stood silent and waiting.

"About those horses. . . ."

"I told you out on the range you'd made more than enough off the stage robbery."

"That don't cut any ice as far as the horses are concerned. I've got half the sale price coming from those animals and I mean to get it."

John studied the face, the whipcord body, tied-down gun, and thin, long hands. He sighed. "It's spent, Jack. All gone."

The outlaw swore quietly, with no special menace. "You figuring on making it up?"

John scowled. "I can't say right now. It depends. Maybe I will and maybe I won't."

"You will, all right."

John nodded solemnly. "Maybe, maybe not. I'm not going to lie about it. Right now I've got bigger things on my mind."

A bleak smile touched the outlaw's mouth, lingered there, low. "Bigger to you, maybe, but what's mine I get. Don't make any mistakes there, John."

"I won't. What did Smalley say?"

"What *didn't* he say. Madder'n a gut-shot boar." The outlaw moved as far as an overhang post, leaned there. "That's my ace in the hole. You fault me, John, and all I have to do is say your name. He'll have you killed in a minute."

"That's nothing I don't know."

"Then you'd best make up your mind what you're going to do, because I don't aim to hang around Vacaville, waiting. Places to go, things to be done."

"I'll make it up," John said, and left the outlaw in the shadows looking after him.

In his room at the Eagle Hotel he pulled a chair up to the window, leaned back in it, and cocked his feet up on the windowsill. Beyond the town lay a westering roll of countryside fading into the night far off. Sounds swarmed up the wooden front of the hotel and were lost in the overhead void where the shadows lived. In some back road a dog fight was in progress. Closer, a muleteer trumpeted near profanity at his animals and a gargantuan rumble of iron tires grinding flinty soil to powder shivered through the atmosphere.

Like the old story of the fly in the spider web, and he was the fly. But he could escape. Go downstairs, cross to the livery barn, saddle up, and disappear into the night. Easy. Ride north to Wyoming. Farther, up to the Broken Arrow outfit in Montana where they knew John Hawk. Or south. Down the dark lanes that led into Mexico, like Jack Keeney had done.

But he'd made the bedroll. No one had forced him to it. He'd made it because he'd wanted it. Then he'd sleep in it. So why in the devil's name had he told Joyce Porter about the Bosworth horses? He could have talked all night without mentioning that. Something about being with her had drawn it out, maybe, and all the telling had done was add more miles to the distance between them. Oh, hell!

He made a cigarette, kicked off his boots, and lay upon the bed fully clothed, gun digging relentlessly into his flesh. There were disadvantages to this complicated kind of life, he thought, and longed wistfully for the existence he'd led for fifteen uncomplicated years. Without trouble, without worries, without fears. Stubbed out the cigarette and slept fully clothed.

And the following morning, when he met Jameson, the liveryman showed no signs of his night-before debauch, was as amiably insincere as ever. They went together to the lawyer's cubbyhole office. John parted with $600, got back a thin piece of paper littered with redundant phraseology, and emerged into the sunshine part owner of the Vacaville-Springerville Stage Company.

He spent the rest of the morning and early afternoon going over the inventory with Cleve and was absorbed enough in what he was doing to forget the things that preyed inside his mind. Until Cleve said: "Mister Keeney said he might consider a steady job with the line, Mister Hawk."

"Who's Mister Keeney?"

Cleve blushed and looked surprised. "The gun guard you sent down with the note."

"Oh, him, yeah." And John turned back to the papers over which he was leaning at the counter and printed words merged, would no longer come up to him off the paper. "He did, did he? Well, I'm not sure we need another guard."

"As an alternate, perhaps?"

John curled up a cigarette, lit it, and looked across at Cleve. "Maybe. We'll worry about that later. Cleve, what's this invoice here for a new Red River stage? There's no such stage here, or if there is, I haven't seen it."

Cleve crossed to the counter, took the invoice, and studied it. He nibbled at his upper lip, sucking it inward. "I've never seen this before, John." He looked up in timid perplexity. "Where did you get this?"

"In that box over there, the one with CJ painted on it."

Cleve's breath erupted hollowly. He grew pale. "Oh, but that's Mister Jameson's private file. Uh . . . we aren't supposed to touch that . . . ever."

"No lock on it and I didn't know." He gazed at the little box and a thought came. "Let me see that again, Cleve."

The clerk handed the invoice back as though delighted to be rid of it. It was imprinted with a seal that said in block letters *Paid.* John read the specifications but what held his attention longest was the date. The stage had been bought from a traveling salesman the evening before. Ordered, bought, and paid for. He was perplexed. Why had Jameson bought a stage without mentioning it? Why had he bought one at all? The line's records showed no need for any additional equipment. In fact there was barely enough business to keep busy the two stages they had on the run, and except for the mail contract. . . .

He put the invoice down upon the counter and a black thought came to him.

"Cleve, when's our mail contract come up for renewal?"

"Mister Jameson and I were looking at that last night. It's due for another round of bidding in three weeks."

"One more question. Has Jameson ever had a partner in here before?"

"Yes, two of them. One went to. . . ."

"Thanks, Cleve," John said with a bitter sound in his voice. Then he smiled at the clerk. "I'm learning, Cleve, learning. There's sure a world of difference between being a rider and a businessman, isn't there?"

"Well, I don't know. I've never. . . ."

"All right. I reckon it's time for me to take off my gloves and pitch in, isn't it?"

Cleve looked at John in uneasy silence.

The big man pushed his hat back and laughed shortly. "I expect the same boot that fits Jameson will fit me, won't it?"

"I don't understand, John."

"Forget it. Just some stray thoughts, Cleve. Something I've wanted to tell you. You've got ideas about what would make the line better, I know. Well, spit 'em out."

"No, I'm just the clerk here. It isn't my. . . ."

"I guess I was too blunt for you. I'll put it this way. I'm in this thing to make money. Make a good living. I don't know a damned thing about it and don't pretend to. I want your ideas, and if they fetch in business, you'll get a raise in pay. How's that sound to you?"

"Mister Jameson doesn't like. . . ."

"Mister Jameson can go suck eggs. If he's what I think he is . . . what I'm *beginning* to think he is . . . why then I don't expect he'll be around here very much, and that'll leave it up to you and me. I guess I'm asking for your help, Cleve. How about it?"

The clerk was scarlet-faced; his hands moved upon the desk like dying birds. "Maybe I could write out some ideas," he said, and John didn't laugh at the timidity, just nodded in silence with the sounds of the evening stage coming to him through the open doorway. Then he heard Ford Tull's high, triumphant yell.

"Do that. Write it all out if you want to and put it in the guard's pigeonhole."

"Yes, I'll do that, John."

Outside the sky was a burnished brass color. Easterly was a bank of great, dirty clouds, God's washing hung to dry. Dogs barked as the coach came wheeling in doing its proud and lurching waddle, wide around the farthest corner of Vacaville. John watched it, sensed pride in something he'd never felt before.

And when the hostlers were working at the horses' heads, he watched the guard climb down nimbly on the far side. Ford Tull descended upon the plank walk side, longhorn mustache curled into an arrogant and lilting bristle.

"Hullo, John Hawk," said the substitute gun guard, coming up. The lean figure was slouched and humor lay, flat and bold, in Jack Keeney's eyes. He had the battered company carbine drooping from beneath his right elbow.

John's mind stumbled, gazed down at the obstacle, and stood fascinated so that his answer was slower coming. "Hello, Jack. How was the run?"

"Fine." The twinkle showed. "I know every switchback and walk-up hill on the run, now." And he laughed softly, meaningfully.

"Put up the carbine and eat supper with me."

"All right."

John waited, big and immovable in the center of the plank walk. He examined the thought that had come to him and shook it loose of kinks until it was the most rational thing he'd known in several days. When Keeney returned, they crossed through the furry dust to the little restaurant beside the Eagle Hotel and John went past the counter to a rickety table in the corner of the room. There was a dirty window on his right.

They ordered food and coffee, and John made a cigarette, left the makings on the table, and smoked a moment under Jack's questioning look.

"What's on your mind, John . . . the horses?"

"Not the horses, a stage line."

Keeney took up the makings and worried up a thick cigarette. He said—"Oh."—and snapped a match, looking up. "There're a dozen better spots than I picked the other night."

"I don't mean robbing it," John said. "I mean owning it."

"What?"

"Owning the line," and he told the outlaw of his half interest. Told where the $600 had come from. Jack Keeney's cigarette went out, pointed straight ahead between motionless fingers. He listened in an expressionless way. ". . . So there's still forty-four hundred dollars due Jameson."

"Whoa up, John. Are you driving at me to put up money from what I got the other night?"

"That's exactly what I'm driving at."

"And paying this Jameson feller off?"

"That's right."

Jack lit his dead cigarette and leaned upon the table. Neither of them spoke until after the food had been left upon the table, then the outlaw began to shake his head in a wry, wagging way. "I'll be gone to hell," he said, "if you aren't a real ring-tailed roarer. Rob me, hire me as guard on the line I robbed, then ask me to use the same money to buy the line from an honest businessman."

"That's what I haven't told you yet. Jameson isn't honest. He knows the mail contract runs out next month. Now then, last night . . . after he knew I was buying in . . . he secretly bought a brand new Red River coach."

"Well?"

"What's he buying coaches for if he's going to let me run the line while he runs his barn?"

"I'm listening."

"Because he aims to bid against me on the mail haul. Break his own line so he can get it back for nothing and my six hundred dollars is gone."

"Whose six hundred dollars?"

"*Our* six hundred dollars, then."

"And how do you know he's up to all this?"

"Feel it. I know his type. Besides that he was going over the mail contract last night with the clerk."

Keeney dropped his cigarette, ground it under a boot heel. "Know what I think, John Hawk? I think outlawing's a hell of a lot simpler'n being in business. Returns are better, too."

"I never saw a businessman hanging from a tree limb, though."

Jack leaned back thoughtfully. "And that's funny, isn't it? Crookeder'n all get-out but protected by the law."

"Very funny."

"Just one thing's funnier. Two outlaws buying a stage line with the line's money . . . or somebody's, anyway." And Keeney laughed in his quiet way. "I've been in some peculiar situations, but this one takes the gold belt."

"You got seven thousand dollars, didn't you?"

Keeney nodded without speaking.

"You'd still have twenty-six hundred left."

"Yeah."

"Well?"

"God, I don't know, John Hawk. You cut off my wind every time I get around you. Damnedest feller I ever saw . . . ever knew."

"Just say yes or no."

"And if it's no?"

John looked down at his cold food. "I'll have to sweat over something else, I reckon."

"Any other ideas?"

"Not along this line, no."

"What then? What other kind do you have?"

"A few for building up the line. Improving business. Making more money out of it."

"Honest money, eh?"

"Yes."

Jack picked up his knife and fork, held them poised over his plate. "All right, John. This is the craziest damned thing I ever heard of, but you got a partner."

CHAPTER FOUR

Jack Keeney brought the money to the office the following day. He and John went to the attorney with instructions for him to pay off John's promissory note and bring it to them. Then they went to the nearby restaurant, and while they waited for service, John pointed out a hurrying Curt Jameson on the far plank walk. Keeney grunted.

"The lawyer's been to see him. Sure looks steamed up, don't he?"

"Let him steam," John said, and bent over his plate. "Now, there are a couple of other things we've got to do. One of us ought to go down to Raton and see how these mail contracts are bid on. See if maybe we can't make a friend or two down there."

"I lived in Raton for ten years," Jack said, chewing.

"But are you wanted down there?"

"No, sir. They knew me as a rancher, those days. Six drought years right in a row finished me off."

"Then maybe you could do what's got to be done down there."

"I might," Jack said. "I used to have lots of friends in Raton."

"And you could find out for sure if Jameson's bidding."

"I expect I could. But there's something sticking in my craw."

John's eyes twinkled as he looked up. "Let me guess . . . those Bosworth horses."

"Nope, not right now anyway. It's Jeff Smalley."

"What about him?"

"He knows me pretty well."

"What of it?"

Jack shrugged. "I don't know, exactly," he said, "only I've got no idea how he'll react to me buying into a business in his town. He could set the law on me, you know."

John leaned back, studied the lean face. "I expect we'd both best steer clear of Smalley," he said. "So far I've had no business with him."

"But you will. He pretty well runs things hereabouts."

"I've heard that before."

Jack nodded slightly. "Wait a little," he said, "and you'll *know* it. Up to now you've just been a stage company gun guard. Now you're edging up a little. You'll meet Jeff."

"What should I know about him?"

"He's as hard as a cannonball, got plenty brains, and snow water for blood. He's got a couple gun hands he keeps around as pets." Jack paused over his plate. "I'd say there's damned little outlawry happens hereabouts he isn't connected with one way or another."

"All right, I'll remember. Now this other job, Jack. While you're in Raton, I'm going to put some notions of mine to work."

"Go ahead. What are they?"

"For one thing those coaches are going to be kept clean. I'll put signs in them about spitting out the windows and rough language. We need passengers. Jameson let the line exist on its mail contract. From now on we can't depend on that."

"No," Jack said, "not until the bidding's over with anyway. And I suppose, even if we get it back, we'll still want passengers. Now, when d'you reckon I ought to head for Raton?"

"Right now. As soon as you're finished with your coffee. It's a long road."

Keeney blinked, set the cup down. "All right. I'll roll my hoop within the hour. You going to ride guard while I'm gone?"

"Yes."

After Jack had left Vacaville, John met Curt Jameson at the company office. The liveryman had a squint-eyed look for him. His mouth was pressed tightly, and a smile of greeting was quickly disposed of.

"Paid off the note, huh? Kidding me when you said you only had six hundred to invest."

"I didn't say that."

Jameson became ingratiating. "You know what I mean," he said. "It amounted to the same thing."

Cleve cut widely around them, heading for the sheds out back where the hostlers stayed. A scent of trouble, disagreeableness in the air frightened him. And John's face was coldly unpleasant.

Jameson ignored the clerk. "That's fine," he said. "That's fine. Now you've got a real stake. That'll be good for both of us. And I won't bother you, John. Lord knows the barn takes all my time anyway. So run this like it was all yours, boy. It'll all be up to you. Won't be any interference from me at all."

John watched Jameson leave the office blank-faced. *Run it like it was your own. . . .* He grew sardonic. *Sure, so that fat, cigar-sucking old fraud could come around after he'd broken the line, taken away its mail contract backbone, and say John had ruined it by bad management. Like it was your own. . . .*

So, for the next ten days John worked as he'd never worked before. He had no time to reflect on Jameson or anyone else—well, almost, during the daylight hours anyway—until a brightness of a kind emerged from the dust and changes he'd wrought. Little printed signs inside both coaches. Scrupulously kept schedules. Changes among the hostlers, the hangers-on. And the greaser was given two additional dollars a week for the added chore of washing each coach when it came in off its run.

Time flowed with a rhythm of unending labor out of which John drew exhaustion and a particular satisfaction from achievement. He ate when he could and slept fitfully, briefly. He revised the line's system of bookkeeping with Cleve hovering close to him. He waded through details as though they were paper leg irons, and ten days later was leaning upon the counter reading a letter from Jack Keeney, postmarked from Raton, when two men entered the office. He turned, recognized the shorter, well-dressed man instantly.

"My name's Smalley. I own the Running Horse down the road." A thick, stubby hand was extended.

"I'm John Hawk. Glad to meet you."

They shook and Smalley acted as though his companion weren't there at all. Lankier, droop-lidded, the second man leaned upon the counter indolently reading a schedule that lay there. His gun was on the left side.

Smalley studied John openly and interestedly. "Curt told me you'd bought into the line. Thought we'd best get acquainted."

"Glad you came by."

"Looks like you're making some changes. Well, progress is a good thing."

"A few changes," John conceded, wondering and waiting.

"I believe a friend of mine is in with you."

"Oh?"

"Feller named Jack Keeney."

"He is. A silent partner, the lawyer calls him."

"Jack's a fine fellow. Is he around?"

"No, he's not."

"Where is he? I'd like to talk to him."

"I'll tell him when he shows up," John said.

Smalley's bland expression hung up on the corners of his

mouth. He was a blunt-jawed man, thick-necked and massive in a squat and powerful way. "Where is he?" he repeated.

And something stirred in John's mind. A warning. "Went out on a little side trip of his own," he said.

Smalley grew silent, staring. After a moment he turned and walked out. The lanky man followed him and John sniffed. Gunman stuck out all over the younger, taller man.

What was on Smalley's mind? He probably meant to get Jack away from John Hawk. He heard Cleve coming through the rear door and turned toward him.

"Cleve, are Curt Jameson and Jeff Smalley good friends?"

"Well, I've always thought so. They've been pretty close ever since I can remember."

"I see."

"John, one of the hostlers is drunk out there."

"Fire him."

Cleve winced. "Me?" he said.

"Sure."

"But I don't believe that's my. . . ."

"I'll go hunt up another one," John said, and walked out. Cleve was rooted. In dismay he twisted one hand inside the other hand. Anguish congested his face.

John had no trouble finding another hostler. There were the usual run of down-at-the-heels freighters and cowboys on the town. The man he hired was burly and blasphemous with an outthrust jaw and a wild light in his eyes.

Afterward, John went to Murphy's Emporium for a new shirt, and met Joyce. She looked at him uncertainly, until he smiled, then, without smiling, she shook her head at him ever so slightly reprovingly. And his smile widened.

"Could I walk with you a little tonight, ma'am?"

She remained still, silently indecisive.

He said: "Better yet. I'll rent a rig from Jameson and take you for a drive."

Then she said: "I wonder if driving with you will be as eventful as walking with you."

They both smiled ruefully over a shared secret.

"Seven o'clock, ma'am?"

"All right."

A wizened clerk came between them. Over his scantily thatched head John watched her leave the store, and told the man what he wanted, got it, went directly to the tonsorial parlor, bought a shave, haircut, and a bath, then went to his room in the Eagle Hotel and changed.

Out of the second-story window, southward, he could see the office. Over its patched, dingy roof he could also see a little of the yard beyond, raked clean, men moving at their chores.

There was a warm sensation at the sight. He smoked without moving from the window, watching the town lose its daytime vitality, slacken its pace as evening fell. He smoked and thought of Keeney's letter. And smiled grimly. Keeney would be home tomorrow. In the meantime he had written that Jameson had already put in a bid for the Vacaville-Springerville mail contract. And more. The Army was taking bids for transporting service personnel from some fort named Buchanan, down near the California line, which it was inactivating, and Jameson had put in for that, also. The company was listed as Smalley and Jameson Stage & Cartage Company, Vacaville, Arizona Territory.

So the smile stayed grim while the eyes lingered upon the little office across the roadway. Until the sun's last splinters were scattered, smothered by mauve shadows. Then he went down the stairs and across the road, engaged a top buggy with red wheels and yellow running gear, climbed up behind the harnessed horse, lifted the lines, and drove north toward the Porter household.

She was waiting on the porch, and there was a leonine man

with her. John dropped the weight, climbed out, went through the gate and up the walk, studying the older man, knowing it was Judge Porter. When she introduced them, the clasp was warm and strong. And John's smile was broad; he'd come this far. Judge Porter hadn't turned away. Had had no reason to turn away. It was for these little, insignificant-appearing things he'd plunged into peril with both eyes open. Not entirely, perhaps, but still. . . .

Then they were down by the buggy and he handed her up, put the weight upon the floorboards, climbed in beside her, and drove off with the distant, faint call of some boys coming down the coolness to them.

John drove aimlessly, remembering how the road had run northward from the days when he'd come down it to Vacaville, and the girl beside him said nothing for so long he turned to see. She was leaning back, watching the darkness loom up, then slide away rearward.

"You're pretty done up in thoughts, aren't you?"

"Yes, the same ones. They don't lessen." She turned to face him. "Aren't you afraid?"

"Sure," he said. "Only I've lived with it so long now I've come to sort of accept it as part of what I'm doing."

"It shouldn't be that way, though."

"Maybe not," he said, "but that doesn't change anything."

"And I'm an accessory."

"A what?"

"An accessory. A person who has helped a criminal."

"You haven't helped me," he said quickly. "Not with the crime."

"But I haven't told about you, either, and that's the same as helping you, Mister Hawk."

"John. Just plain John. And I know you haven't."

"But what will happen? We can't just go on forever knowing

what we know and doing nothing about it."

"Other people have," he said.

"I couldn't and I don't believe you could, either. If you could have, why did you tell me?"

He watched the big horse pick its stolid way along the faint tracks. "I guess because I like to talk to you. And I didn't like having a secret. You can't build friendships on secrets."

"I wish you hadn't told me," she said, and looked straight ahead.

The buggy rocked gently, red wheels making rustling sounds against the dusty earth. Far ahead a straight pillar of pale white stood vertically in the sky. He watched it, knowing it wasn't a fire, but rather a fire's reflection. A big fire at that. He sighed.

"What should I do, do you think?"

"Pay for them."

"What with?"

She looked briefly at him. "I have no idea."

"I put everything I had into the stage company."

"Couldn't you repay it over a period of time?"

"I don't know." He reached down for the lines, drew the buggy off the road toward a dark and cool clump of trees, drove in among them, and stopped. They were upon a slight eminence. Far off eastward a cordillera lay. Above it, like a ridge of gristle, was a pale glow that separated the ridges and peaks from the night.

And northwest was the glow of a bonfire. He watched it with a frown lying between his eyes. "What's that?"

"A brush fire," she answered. "The cattlemen drag a big chain between two teams of horses and break up the brush. They pile it up, and when the nights are a little damp, they burn it. It clears the range."

"Oh."

She moved a little on the seat, and the buggy squeaked. "Let me try an idea I have."

He sighed, still looking at the fire. "All right. What is it?"

"I know Mister Bosworth. He and my father were raised together. I'll find out what the horses were worth, and if he'll take repayment over a period of months."

He bent, looped the lines about the whip socket, then leaned back. "Well, first off he'll want to know why you're interested, and secondly he'll want to know who you're doing it for."

"No, I don't think so. Franklin Bosworth is like an uncle to me. He won't ask any questions or tell my father. I'm sure of it."

"Then he's an unusual man," John said.

"He is. And that's only one more reason why I believe he deserves decency . . . honest treatment. Then there's that seven thousand dollars. . . ."

He gazed at her and for a moment assimilation kept him still and silent, then he said: "And you think I may have had a hand in that, too, don't you?"

"I don't think either way. I just *hope* you didn't."

"I can give you my word on that. I had nothing to do with it at all."

"Then let me work the horse stealing out with Franklin Bosworth."

"Why? I mean besides Bosworth . . . why?"

"Why?" she said. "Because letting it lie dormant is as wrong as doing it in the first place was. That's why."

"Oh."

"I'll ride up there tomorrow. It'll be a relief to do it. To stop thinking about it."

"I guess I shouldn't have worried you with it," he said.

She made a short gesture with her hands and fell silent.

"But don't say I'll give more than a hundred dollars a month because that's all I can pay right now." He made a cigarette, dwelt over it meticulously. "Even that's going to cripple me a little."

"I thought the stage company paid you well."

"It does," he said, inhaling, exhaling, "but I'm only planning on taking a guard's pay. The rest of the money I want to plow back into the company. Build it up that way, you see."

"Oh. I don't know much about business."

He smiled around at her. "Me, too. The more I learn, the less I know."

She didn't return the smile but leaned back like he was doing and heard the night all around them. They heard the dull and persistent *clop-clop* of a horse coming up from the south, from the direction of Vacaville.

John leaned out to see the traveler. The animal was trudging along placidly, and just as he began to draw his head back, the rider stopped, bent low from the saddle, and peered at the ground where they had turned off. He lifted the reins, bent them, and the horse resumed its shambling walk, following the buggy tracks toward the little hilltop. John's interest sharpened. Without turning, he said: "We're going to have a visitor. Did you tell anyone we might come up this way?"

"No. I had no idea which way we were going."

He twisted lightly, dropped to the ground beside the buggy, and watched. Joyce was pale in the buggy's darkness.

"John?"

"Be quiet," he said, with hair rising along the base of his skull. "Sit still. I'm going to move off a little." And he did, going in a sidling way toward the deeper shadows where tree trunks were.

The stranger's reins were swinging, his horse traveling head-down, carelessly. The man himself was tall, lanky, faceless, and nearly indistinguishable. When he drew close enough to make out the buggy, he stopped, gazed at the rig a moment, then swung down, left his horse, and moved gently forward at an angle.

And John knew fear. It snugged up around his heart like a hang rope, and tightened. He recognized the silhouette without knowing the man. Smalley's companion of earlier who wore a left-handed gun.

The moving shadow got fairly close before it stopped with its head tilted back a little.

"Hawk!"

John watched, saying nothing.

"Hawk, come out of the buggy!"

The rig squeaked as Joyce moved and John's mouth flattened in the darkness by the trees. "What do you want?" he asked softly.

The stranger grew stiff, seemed surprised at the direction John's reply came from. He turned ever so slightly. "Come out where I can see you, Hawk."

"Who are you and what do you want?"

"Never mind who I am, just do like I say. Is the girl up there with you? If she is, send her out fifty feet ahead of you."

John drew his gun, cocked it quietly, and said: "Joyce, stay where you are."

"Oh," the long, thin shadow said, "so she's in there. That's all the better. Now then, Hawk, walk out of those trees. Come on."

"Come in here after me, mister," John invited with certainty in him as solid as stone. "Why didn't Smalley come himself?"

The assassin made no reply. He seemed to be weighing chances, advantages. None was in his favor. He was visible and John was not. His voice was strangely detached and cool-sounding. "Come on out, Hawk. I want to talk to you."

"Talk, hell," John said bluntly. "You weren't sent up here to talk. Not your type."

"Yes I was," the gunman said in the same quiet, drawling

73

way. "Are you coming out of them trees or not?"

"No."

"Then I'm coming in."

And he began to walk in a leisurely way toward the darkest shadows. When he passed the buggy, Joyce strained to see him. The night was too black.

When he was close enough, John halted him with a sharp word. He stood still, waiting, and when John appeared gun in hand, he even smiled a little.

"Ready for anything, aren't you?" The gunman was heavy-eyed and hatchet-faced with Texas sticking out all over him, Texas killer.

"What do you want?"

"Jeff sent me after you with a message. You're to stick to the passenger business and leave mail contracts alone."

John stood in resolute silence, making out the face before him. In a low and quiet way he said: "All right, you've told me. Anything else?"

The killer's heavily lidded eyes dropped to the pointing gun. "No," he said in the same detached way. "I never argue with the drop. In fact, I never argue at all unless fellers like you make it necessary. *Adiós.*"

John holstered his gun when the head-down horse was walking southward again, bearing its tall burden. Then he crossed to the buggy where Joyce's eyes caught him, held him with their liquid sheen of fear.

"What did he mean? Are you bidding on a mail contract, John?"

"I aim to, yes, but haven't done it yet. The Vacaville-Springerville contract. The company has it now." He told her the entire story, even what Jack Keeney had written him from Raton.

"Jeff Smalley," she said softly. "I told you about him once."

"I remember." He unlooped the lines as though to drive back. She brushed fingers across his forearm.

"Wait. Not just yet."

He sat patiently, looking at her. She was white and frightened and her mouth was a straight, harsh line.

"All this trouble . . . is it worth it, John?"

Looking steadily into the moving depths of her eyes, he nodded. "Yes, I'd say it was, Joyce. It's probably worth it all right, but even if it wasn't . . . even if it was just the stage company and nothing else . . . why, then I expect they've put me into a position where a man das'n't back down."

"There's the law. . . ."

He recalled Jameson's scorn. Other things he'd heard, fragments, innuendoes. Jeff Smalley, ex-lawman of Vacaville, boss of it all. Thinking of her father, he said: "Maybe, but the law can't do anything until a crime's been committed."

"Threatening you is a crime."

He drew the lines slowly through his fingers, frowning at them. "My word against his and he'd have a dozen witnesses to say that he wasn't up here at all."

"I saw him."

"No, you aren't mixed up in this. You can't be."

He raised the lines, flipped them. The big horse moved out, made a large circle, and went obediently toward the roadway, southward toward Vacaville.

"It seems unreal," she said when they were finally on the outskirts of town. "All of it."

"I guess it does. Now, about those Bosworth horses. . . . Maybe you'd better not say anything about them just yet."

She was watching him closely and he knew it when she said: "Why?"

"Well, if you make it look like you know who stole them and anything happens that I can't pay Bosworth, why everyone'll just naturally insist you tell them what it's all about. Probably your father'll even find out."

"What might happen?"

He shrugged. "I'm just thinking ahead, that's all."

"Smalley might have you ambushed, John, or something like that?"

"Don't be digging, Joyce," he said. "Let's just let things ride for a spell and see what happens."

When the rig cut in by the Porter house, he helped her down. He took her to the gate and stood across it from her, conscious of its barrier-like thickness. In charged words she said: "I won't, John. I won't just stand by and watch this . . . this attack on you by all those others. I simply refuse. . . ."

"What can you do about it?"

"Tell my father," she said with a flashing look.

"Listen, Joyce," he said patiently. "That would be the worst thing you could do. Don't you see that?"

"No, why would it?"

"Because he'd go to Smalley's law, that's why."

"Smalley's law?"

"Sure. I've heard that ever since I came down here. Jeff Smalley owns Vacaville's law. He says who is to be arrested and who isn't to be arrested. If your father went to Smalley's law in an effort to protect me, he'd stir things up and for a while I'd like them to just sort of coast along."

"But you haven't any plans."

He smiled at her. "I'm making them right now. In fact, I was making them on the way home tonight, so let sleeping dogs lie until I see you again . . . please?"

She started to say something, then didn't. Her hands resting on the gate were closed around it tightly. "Good night," she said, and hurried up the walk.

He drove the rig back to Jameson's barn and left it. He was

too wide-awake for sleep, so he by-passed the Eagle Hotel and went to the stage company office instead. Letting himself into the office, he dropped wearily into a chair, cocked his feet up, and made a cigarette.

Vacaville's night noises came distantly to him. He catalogued them mentally without conscious effort. Until he heard a commotion in the yard behind the office and got up slowly, went to the rear door, unlocked it, and threw it wide.

Moonlight was spread flat-white across the yard. Over near the alternate coach were two figures. One was the sniffling greaser, the other was the burly man he'd recently hired. They were arguing. He heard the shivering boy say: "I'll get fired, not you."

He stepped out into the yard and crossed it.

The boy saw him first, stiffened, looking past the man. "What's the trouble?"

The big man turned then but neither of them answered. Closer, John saw that a rear burr was off the alternate coach's near-side rear wheel. Glimmering in the moonlight were steel filings adhering to the viscous axle grease. John went around the man and boy, bent and looked, then straightened up with cold understanding, anger building up.

"Who did that?"

The boy looked at the ground. The burly man returned John's stare without speaking.

He went up to them. "I asked who put those filings in there."

The boy shuffled his feet in agony and looked at the hostler. John stretched out his arm. The hostler's movement was quick. He struck the arm aside and moved back. John gestured to the boy.

"Get out of the way."

The boy sidled backward in an ungainly way. John looked steadily at the hostler. The man was unarmed and in his undershirt, pants, and boots. Apparently he'd arisen in the late hours to put the damaging filings into the grease and the boy had inadvertently come upon him.

"Why did you do that? Who told you to do it?" John knew the answer before the echo of his voice died away. The hostler was watching him malevolently, as silent as a rock.

"I guess I've had enough," John said. "More'n enough."

For a large man he was surprisingly fast. The first blow caught the hostler moving, drew a coughing curse out of him, drove him off balance.

Then John went to work. The boy was transfixed. He shivered when blows landed in the moonlight, in the long, electric silence of the yard. And finally he rushed toward the bunkhouse, mouth askew, ugly, and upset-looking, to rouse the other hired hands, for this was truly a battle between giants.

John was slow dodging a solid smash that hurt him, high in the chest and to one side so that he had to back away, covering, watching the heavier man rushing in for his kill. Then he straightened up and fired a withering slam that brought Smalley's man up short. Set him rocking stupidly, arms down.

He moved in closer, struck the thick body at will. Planted blows where he wanted to but the hostler wouldn't crumble. Backing up, he measured his man, shuffled in to slide beneath a blind swing, and loosed a terrible strike that caught the big hostler in the face, forced his head back with a sickening snap. The hostler dissolved, fell inward in a heap. Dark stains spread in the dust. Moonlight shone off them like ink, wet and shiny and black.

John could feel his hands swelling. His side hurt from that thunderous blow and he breathed shallowly. He saw three white faces peering at him. Puffy faces, tousled hair as still as death. Eyes that brimmed with hot excitement. The greaser was closest.

"Did you see him putting those filings in there?"

The boy nodded, fascinated by the ruin in the dust, never taking his eyes off it. "Yes, sir, Mister Hawk. I seen him doing it, and when I come up, he said he'd break my neck if I told anybody."

"Listen, fellers," John said, not without trouble for his breath was short, heart pounding in his ears. "Listen to me. I know why he was doing that. I want each of you to know that if any of you sell out to anyone who wants the coaches ruined or the horses crippled, I'll hunt you down and what this *hombre* got won't hold a candle to what you'll get. I mean it. Every damned word of it. So remember it, you fellows. If you want to quit, that's fine, but don't try anything like this man tried. I'm warning you right now. All right. Do any of you want to quit?"

Each of them said no. Their faces showed a mounting curiosity but none asked why the filings had been put there. By whose orders. It was enough for them, at that moment, to know that it had been done. Other questions would find expression later for such is the way with small minds.

John started back toward the office, veered off at a water trough, and held his bruised hands in the cold water for a while. The anger died slowly and bitterness replaced it. Calculatingly cold bitterness. The kind that bends every effort to the cause of retaliation.

He went back into the office and made another cigarette. He stood in the shadows smoking, watching the lights go out here and there. Down the road at the Running Horse was muffled raucousness. He stared in that direction for a long time before he left the office, locked the door, and flipped the cigarette away.

He walked across the road and turned into the doorway of the Eagle Hotel when two men went shuffling past. He heard one say: ". . . to buy hay for Jameson tomorrow. What you got to do?"

The other man's answer was lost in a burst of shouts from the saloon. John trudged up the stairs to his room, entered, groped for the lamp, and when his fist was closing around it the idea came to him. He stayed motionlessly in that bent position with darkness pressing in upon him.

And finally went to bed in the darkness. Only he laid wide-awake, thinking, evolving a plan that would be dependent upon Jack Keeney's arriving home on the morrow. Then he slept.

Late morning brought Keeney to the office, wearing a crooked smile, beard stubble, and travel-stained clothing. John yelled for Cleve, gave him money, and sent him out for food and coffee. Then he told Jack of the incident of steel filings in the axle grease, and Jack in turn told him what he'd learned in Raton.

They talked until noon. Jack finished his breakfast and coffee, rubbed the stubble, and said he'd go get a shave.

"And after that, get a fresh horse and ride the back country with your twenty-six hundred dollars."

Jack arose, stretched mightily, and yawned. "All right, but, man, you're sure using up my money fast." He went out, keeping a weather eye toward the Running Horse, for they'd concluded that the best strategy for them both would be to avoid Smalley and Smalley's gunmen, at least for the time being.

John remained in the office with glum thoughts, and when Cleve came diffidently in from the rear yard, John's nod was subdued. He watched Cleve go to his desk.

"Cleve, did you fire that drunk?"

A darting look, a blush. "Yes."

"I fired one last night myself. It's not so hard, is it?" Cleve was uncomfortable. He said tentatively: "Well, no. . . ."

Out in the road an exuberant cowboy raised a shrill yell that hung in echoless vibrancy for a second, and died. Cleve started and John saw it. He thought about it for a moment before he arose at the sound of the stage coming in from Springerville, then an appalling thought struck him.

"Good Lord! I was supposed to ride guard."

Cleve cleared his throat, shuffled some papers on his desk. "I took care of that," he said. "I came down early to check out the load and passengers and you weren't here. . . . I asked my brother to go this one time, and he did."

John gazed at the timid man in silence, then started for the door. Why had the Lord seen fit to saddle a man of Cleve's staunchness with a rabbit's courage?

Vacaville was shaking off drowsiness. The stage came up with its high-twisting dust. Rolled to the plank walk and reeled back. Ford Tull hurled a gloved fist beneath his magnificent mustache and winked broadly at John. From ten feet in the air he was lord of all he saw.

And loping easily far up the north end of Vacaville's wide roadway Jack Keeney rode straight and tall in the saddle, whistling a mournful song that came faintly down the hushed roadway.

John turned and watched his partner rein westward and disappear beyond the farthest jumble of shacks.

CHAPTER FIVE

The following day two events transpired that pleased John, leavened his mood. One, the attorney brought his promissory note back, cancelled. The lawyer was shorter than average with a fox-like face and sad, dark eyes. Informing John the cancellation had been duly recorded, he put the note upon the counter.

"But what surprised me," he said, "was that Jameson was glad to get the money . . . which is understandable of course . . . only most men like him want interest and not the principal."

John gazed at the note. "Maybe his reasons are different from most men's," he said, then burned the note with Cleve watching. He let it fall into a wastebasket as it curled into black flakes. The lawyer didn't view the act with approval but he kept silent until the last shred disintegrated.

"Well, Mister Hawk, if you need me again, stop by."

"Thanks."

The second pleasing event was when Jack Keeney returned late in the afternoon. John greeted him with the suggestion he ride guard on the dawn stage south. Keeney squinted through swollen eyes.

"Say, did you own slaves before the war?" he asked acidly, and fell into a chair.

"You can guess why I don't want you around, Jack."

Keeney began to worry up a cigarette. He nodded without enthusiasm. "All right. And I come back tomorrow night?"

"Nope."

Keeney looked into the steady eyes a moment, then licked the cigarette, folded it, closed, and lit it. "Well, now what?" he said.

"Stay down at Springerville for a few days, Jack. Hire us a new gun guard down there, too. One that doesn't know Smalley or Jameson and who'll use a gun if he has to."

"So I'll be out of the way, eh?"

"Yes."

"Hell," Jack said. "They'll hear I'm down there."

"Maybe by that time we won't have the cougar by the tail any more."

"Suits me," Jack said, winking at Cleve. "I'll sleep for a month."

"How'd you make out today?"

"Bought all I could find that was for sale."

"Good. Another thing, Jack. Can those mail people down in Raton be bought?"

Jack shook his head emphatically. "Not a chance in this world," he said. "Two of them are sons of old friends of mine. They turned to stone when I hinted about the contract. Civil, you understand, but as cold as ice where advance information was concerned."

"Then Jameson and Smalley'll have no better chance than we'll have."

Jack inspected the end of his cigarette. "I wouldn't say that," he said. "They know the ropes about bidding and we don't, but as far as underhandedness goes, they won't get to scratch."

"You said you'd learned about the bidding."

"I have learned about it, only they've been at it before and I haven't. That means something, John."

"Well, would it help any, if you stayed down there next week, or until the contracts are put up for bid?"

Jack shook his head. "I don't believe so," he said. "I figured to go back the day before we bid. If I went back today, I wouldn't know any more'n I already know."

John was silent a moment. Jack smoked in silence.

John arose, moved around the office, passed Cleve's desk without looking at the clerk. While the conversation lagged, a loose-running gust of air blew against the building. It had a metallic smell, an autumnal taste to it.

Cleve cleared his throat. "John, do you recall that invoice for a new Red River coach you found in Mister Jameson's strong-box?"

"Yes."

Cleve's hands were locked together. "I heard some riders in the café last night talking about seeing a coach like that up at Ahern, about thirty miles north of here."

Jack looked from one to the other, shifted in his chair in order to get a better view of the clerk.

"That's interesting," John said, saw Jack's quizzical expression, and explained.

The outlaw listened, slouched like a half-empty grain sack in the chair, exhaled a long gust of smoke with his eyes growing remote. "There's considerable mention of equipment in the bid letters," he said. "A successful bidder's supposed to have crack stages and sound horses. Old stuff like ours is permissible, you understand, but the government makes it pretty plain that new equipment is what it'd like all bidders to have." He canted his head at John. "That'll be a feather in Jameson's and Smalley's hat, that new coach."

John sat down again. "They'll have two feathers," he said. "The new coach is one. The fact that Jameson's had the contract before is another." He sighed. "Cleve, would you say our passenger business is good enough to support the line by itself?"

Cleve touched a paper with figures on it, kept his eyes upon the columns when he answered. "I would say the passenger business is growing . . . has been growing quite a bit lately . . . but it wouldn't do more than pay running expenses, John. Right now, anyway."

Jack held out a hand. "Let me see your figures."

John looked, and then handed the paper to Keeney. "And there it is," he said dryly, "in a few sound words."

Jack folded the paper, put it in his shirt pocket, gripped the arms of his chair, preparing to rise. "Then I'd expect something else's got to be done," he said.

"Like what?"

But Keeney was out of the chair and moving toward the door. He waved a hand without answering and disappeared.

Absently Cleve said: "That report of operations had the bid figures on it. How low we dare bid and still make money."

John said: "That's all right. Jack might need it."

By dusk, when the evening stage was ready, Jack was atop the box next to Ford Tull, company carbine lying loosely in the crook of his arm, small eyes holding to the front of the Running Horse Saloon in a brooding, still way.

John stepped atop the fore wheel. "Send me letters by Ford," he said, "and I'll do the same with you."

Jack looked down into John's face. "One more week to go," he said, then added with unusual fierceness: "We've got to win, John. Got to."

The coach hurtled to life with passengers clutching hats, cut a wide swath through a roadway drenched with blood-red, dying sunlight, threw up its own dust banner before disappearing southward.

When John turned back toward the office, a thick arm was thrust stiffly before him. He looked at the face beyond. Sean O'Brien, the dour farrier, was gazing at him stonily.

"Here, this is for you."

John took the note and O'Brien walked abruptly away.

Cleve lingered, seeing John open the paper, then he returned to the office, and John read the note twice before he, too, went inside.

Cleve hung the clip board on a nail in the side of his desk, removed the alpaca sleeve protectors, and smoothed off the top of his desk.

John watched him without seeing the movements. He leaned heavily upon the counter. "Cleve, do you know this Franklin Bosworth fellow?"

"Yes, he's a rancher northeast of town. Has three big sons."

"What kind of a man is he?"

Cleve tidied up a loose stack of papers. "I've always heard he was very upright. I know he's wealthy. It was his money that time, early this summer, that was taken off the Springerville-bound stage. You'd remember, of course. You were riding guard."

"Yeah, I remember. I also remember seeing in his shipping invoice a responsibility clause Jameson had signed."

"That's right. We always sign those clauses insuring delivery of bullion."

"Damned risky, isn't it?"

"Well, yes, but it's customary. All the lines do it. If we didn't, another line'd open a station here, and we'd lose the business."

"Did Jameson make good Bosworth's loss?"

"Oh, yes. I was here when he gave him the full seven thousand dollars. Mister Jameson was upset for several days afterward."

John shoved the crumpled note into a pocket. "Upset? I'll bet he was worse than that." At Cleve's faintest of smiles, he added: "I'll bet his heart nigh stopped. Well, lock up and I'll see you in the morning."

He ate at the café next to his hotel and watched the clock. Later he went upstairs, cleaned up, and returned to the roadway. The evening had a briskness to it. There was even a faint aroma of black-oak smoke. Fall was coming. The stars were brittle-clear, the sky a sharper cobalt color. He walked northward as far as her house and she was standing at the gate, waiting. Her hair was caught up on both sides, swept backward and held at the nape of her neck by a bright green ribbon. Her features were soft and grave, the fullness of her mouth even, lips closed without pressure. He thought she was very beautiful, and she was.

"I got your note."

She passed through the gate, saying: "I suppose everyone knew he hadn't been to Raton since early spring. Would guess from that he still had the money at the ranch."

"When did it happen?"

"Last night."

"Was anyone hurt?"

"Only Mister Bosworth. He was struck over the head . . . nothing serious."

"Well," John said, looking past her at the square of light coming from the Porter parlor window, "let's walk down by the church. Will you be warm enough?"

"Yes."

So they went slowly, wrapped in their thoughts, as far as the huddling building with its frail, slanted cross overhead, and he swiped at the steps with his hat, then dropped down beside her. He leaned back in a withdrawn way, mouth pursed, his mind as crystal-clear as the night air.

Smalley ruled the lawless, and Jameson was Smalley's partner. Jameson had paid Bosworth $7,000 several months back. And Bosworth, foolishly perhaps, but nevertheless as was the custom, had kept the money at his ranch. He'd been robbed. John had no doubts about the crime, only about his position in relation to it. A stranger, a newcomer, an antagonist of Jameson's. . . . He looked around at her. "Well?"

"Who would have done it?" she asked.

She was looking directly at him with a hushed appearance, an expectancy mingled with dread on her face.

"Guessing's not very reliable," he said, "but I could guess."

"John, my father's heard some rumors. They're about you."

"Oh?" he said, affecting a casualness he didn't feel. "What about me?"

"That you have an outlaw for a partner. Another is that you both are wanted men."

"What did your father say?"

"He doesn't put much faith in rumors, but he asked me to stay away from you until things are resolved a little."

"I see," he said, anxiety settling low behind his belt, solidly. "And maybe he's right, Joyce. Maybe you shouldn't see me. Not because I'm wanted . . . which isn't true at all . . . but because of what's ahead."

"John, who *is* your partner?"

"A rider named Keeney."

"Yes," she said quickly, "that's the name, Keeney."

"Jack's had some hard knocks," he said, "and I've never set myself up to judge other people. But if I did, I'd say that Jack Keeney's as honest as half the men in this town."

And she didn't say the natural thing, because she didn't know it was true, that half the men in Vacaville were not too honest.

"Rumors like that," he continued, "are deliberately started to discredit people. You can guess why it's so in my case."

"It would have to do with your trouble over the mail contract, wouldn't it?"

"Yes."

"But there is so *much* trouble lately."

He thought: *It hasn't even begun yet, Joyce.*

"After I heard the rumors, I was afraid people might imagine you had something to do with the Bosworth robbery, John."

"Some probably will," he said. "Everything that's happened

88

since I came here could very easily be laid to the door of a stranger, someone who wasn't raised hereabouts, isn't well known."

"That's it exactly," she said.

He took one of her hands and held it. "Every time I'm with you, there's trouble, Joyce. I imagine how it's going to be, and it never is."

She didn't move.

"It seems as if it isn't someone's cussed stolen horses, then it's a gunman riding up, or a robbery, or something. Just for once I'm going to make out like there's nothing."

"You can't, though," she said, subdued and still.

"Can't I?" His grip tightened a little, spasmodically, almost unconsciously. "Look, see that little crooked cross up there? It's weathered years of storms. Will weather more years of them. Look up farther . . . no, over this way. That winking blue star, my old friend, the North Star. I've been places where he seemed different. Seemed like he'd moved around, gotten behind me some way. Of course he hadn't, but I've been on some pretty far-off trails."

She lowered her gaze to his tilted profile. "Were you always with . . . just men?"

Then his head came down slowly and he was smiling at her. "As a matter of fact, no, not always. There've been cowmen's wives and daughters, schoolmarms, missionary ladies, dance-hall girls. You can't bump around a lot and not run across women, because there are only two kinds of folks . . . men and women." Quite suddenly he released her hand, put it back in her lap. But his smile was as broad as ever.

"But the one I remembered the longest was right here in Vacaville. She's a beauty, too. The kind of a woman who makes men outlaws." At her altering expression he nodded to emphasize what he was saying. "Honest Injun. The kind of a woman that makes a drifter dissatisfied with himself as he's always been."

"I don't think you're being rational," she said.

"Maybe not, but at least I'm being truthful. Someday I'll tell you the whole story. Then you can judge. Right now you couldn't. You're too upset about other things."

She kept looking at him. "Am I that woman?" she asked.

He nodded at her, slowly and without speaking.

Instead of jumping up, or stiffening, or looking disapproving as he'd thought she would, she simply drew up her legs and lowered her head until it rested upon them. The moon glow glistened in her hair, carved deep shadows around the fullnesses of her figure. She was distant in thought and silhouette.

He made a cigarette, lit it, and smelled its added fragrance in the tangy preface to autumn that was around them in the darkness.

"I will have been in Vacaville seven months, pretty soon," he said after a while. "That's a long time."

"No, it's not very long, John. I've been here all my life." She turned her head a little. "It doesn't seem long at all, but it's twenty-two years."

"I've never stayed anywhere more than two years, before."

"Do you want to leave?"

He looked at her through narrowed eyes, smoke twisting up and around them, mushrooming under his hat brim, breaking out. "I think you know the answer to that," he said, "without any answer at all."

She looked away from him again. "What shall I tell my father?"

"About what?"

"About not seeing you."

"Oh." He shifted position a little and blew out a long funnel of smoke. "It's up to you, Joyce."

"He and I've always been very close, John. My mother died when I was born. I couldn't lie to him."

"I wouldn't ask you to."

"He hasn't forbidden me to see you."

John thought of the leonine head, the imperturbable gray eyes. "I didn't size him up as an unfair or demanding man."

"He isn't. He's very understanding. But in this case I think his concern. . . ."

"Is first for you, secondly for your reputation. I know."

She looked at him again. "John, do you know that in your way you're a lot like him. You're much more sensitive to other people than you appear to be."

He removed the cigarette, flicked it, and examined its tip. "To some people," he said. "Just to some people. That's why I'd be willing to bet my horse that Jameson knows about the Bosworth robbery."

"Who committed it?"

"Yes."

"Would Jeff Smalley be implicated?"

"As sure as night follows day," he said, and killed the cigarette. "I'd be as sure of that as I am that they've started those rumors about me. It all fits a pattern, the workings of men being like they are. Jameson, especially, would do that. Tell me something, Joyce. When Jameson had another partner in the stage line, weren't there rumors about him before he went bankrupt, lost out, and left the country?"

"There were a lot of rumors *after* he left. I don't recall any before, but then I probably wouldn't have heard them anyway. My interests then were quite a bit different than they are now. I was still in school."

He stared at his boots a moment, examining an idea. When a man repeats himself, as Curt Jameson was undoubtedly doing, wouldn't knowing what he'd done before, in an earlier and identical case, be helpful?

"Tell me," he said, "exactly what you *do* remember about his other partner, what happened to him. Everything you can remember."

She frowned in concentration, then shrugged. "About all I recall with any clarity is that it was said, after he'd left the country, that he'd participated in a local robbery. A gambler was. . . ."

He jerked erect, interrupting her. The wind came unnoticed and hurried past, touching them only briefly, and was gone down through town.

"What's the matter, John?"

"Why didn't I think of that before?" he asked, and got to his feet, took her arms, and pulled her up, also. "Joyce, Bosworth's robbery was done for seven thousand dollars *and to get me.*"

She stood with her shoulders forward a little, upper arms in his grip.

A wild flag was flying in his eyes, and he smiled a slow, cold smile. "Sure as the devil. Jameson's to get his stage line back and five thousand invested dollars to boot, just like he worked it the other times, and the surest way to be shed of me is to see me placed on a Wanted poster. The other fellows ran and I'd be a fool not to. Smalley is Jameson's partner, and Smalley owns the law. I'd be sent to prison as sure as God made little green apples."

"John. . . ."

"No, just listen for a minute. We'll do like your paw wants. After tonight we won't see each other alone again. I've got reasons, too, now. Jameson and Smalley aren't above getting you hauled into this muck. But I want you to do something for me, and it's important."

"Anything."

"Go see Franklin Bosworth tomorrow. As soon as you can.

Ask him to ride down to see me. Tell him to make it no later than tomorrow. Tell him not to tell anyone he's coming and by no means to let on that he's coming to see *me*. Do you understand?"

"Yes, I understand. I'll go before breakfast. At dawn, in fact. But, John, if he doesn't come. . . ."

"He's got to come, Joyce. Got to, and it's up to you to make him do it."

As it turned out, Franklin Bosworth was perfectly agreeable, although he had no inkling *why* Jameson's new partner wanted to see him. A big, elderly man with three huge sons and a worldliness not otherwise found in the Vacaville country, Bosworth was both warm and easy to know.

When he tied his rig before the stage company office, John saw him through the open door and guessed who he was. He appraised the older man and the two images of him who alighted with him. He asked Cleve to go make a harness check out back and received Bosworth alone.

The rancher's sons were introduced and gazed with frank appraisal at John. One remained by the door, the other took a chair off to one side of the room near a window where he could see in all directions. Bosworth waved a meaty hand deprecatingly.

"Family's sort of skittery since we were robbed. The boys seem to think someone's out for trouble with us. First it was some horses, then seven thousand dollars we lost off a stage, and now this robbery."

John pushed up a chair for the big man. "I know. I was the guard on the stage that your money was on."

"Were you now," Bosworth said, sitting down but looking at John with new interest. "Well then, you must be the man who tracked the highwayman in the dark."

93

"I tracked him to the box, yes," John said, and offered his tobacco sack, which was declined with a kindly shake of the big head. "But since the stage line paid you, I've sort of lost interest in that."

"You weren't a part owner then, I take it," Bosworth said.

John grinned wryly at him. "No, I wasn't." He hadn't anticipated the sons, like listening statues. Their presence shook him. "But that isn't what I wanted to talk to you about."

"No? Something about the robbery, maybe?"

"Not that, either." John took a big drag off his cigarette. "It's about your stolen horses." He saw three sets of eyes come to bear and pushed on. "You must have an idea what those horses were worth to you, by now."

"Well, yes," Franklin Bosworth said slowly. "But to replace them would cost more than I had in them, you understand. Those animals were our select mounts for working cattle, Mister Hawk."

"How much would you say they were worth to you?"

But Bosworth wasn't so simple. He gazed in his imperturbable way at John. "Let me ask you a question," he said. "Why are you concerned?"

John heard the silence, felt it grow leaden and thick around him, throughout the office. "Because, Mister Bosworth, the man who stole them sold them. He now wants to make restitution."

The silence lingered a moment.

"I see." Bosworth had ice-blue eyes. They were unshakably calm and confident. They were also mighty shrewd and measuring. "Well," he said, "you've caught me off balance a little, Mister Hawk."

"I suppose I have. But that's only part of what I want to talk about. If you'll give me an answer, we can get to the next thing."

"Maybe we should go on to that now. Come back to the

horses later. I'll have time to think it over that way."

But John wasn't so disposed, although he smiled at the larger and older man. "I believe we'd better polish this off first. You see, what else is on my mind isn't as simple as stolen horses."

"In that case," Bosworth said without hesitancy, "I'd say the horses were worth seven hundred and fifty dollars to me."

"And would you take restitution?"

Bosworth twisted in the chair, looked at his sons. The older one across the room was staring at John in a still and thoughtful way. He spoke up.

"Mister Hawk . . . would you, by any chance, be the horse thief?"

John returned his stare in spades. "I would be," he said.

The son's eyes brightened, grew sharp and triumphant. He even smiled down around his mouth, without humor. "I'm not surprised," he said. "What surprises me is that a horse thief has a conscience."

His father said: "All right, Tom." Although it was an affable, calm rebuke, the hulking man in the tilted-back chair fell silent.

John stood motionless under Franklin Bosworth's scrutiny. The rancher was silent a long time. "You know, Mister Hawk," he said quietly, "some of those animals were pets of mine." When John neither spoke nor moved, Bosworth's eyes clouded. "Well," he said in a soft yet gruff way, "I'm not God. When a man's in error and admits it, offers to set it to rights, I've never tried to hang him. Now then . . . how can you repay me?"

"One hundred dollars a month, sir."

"Upon your word?"

Conscious of the older son's gaze, which he suspected would now be hard and gloatingly sardonic, John nodded his head. "Upon my word, Mister Bosworth."

"In that case, Mister Hawk, you've just bought sixty-four head of very good working cow horses, and while I hate like the devil to lose them, at my age I'm prouder to meet an honest horse thief." He arose with a smile and pushed out a big hand.

"Wait, Dad," the older boy said without moving from his chair. "He's got more to say."

"Oh, yes," Bosworth said in small confusion, and sat down again.

John gazed at the son in the chair. There was nothing saturnine about the expression he saw, just a speculative and perhaps suspicious regard. A hardness born of inherent confidence and fearlessness but no condemnation. At least not yet anyway.

"The other matter," Bosworth prompted.

John looked back toward him again. "Yes. It's about the robbery." And he heard both sons draw in their breath. This time he saw fierceness in their faces. An unreasoning savagery that he was glad he wasn't going to have to talk his way clear of, for the sons had no mercy in their minds for the man who had assaulted their father.

"What about it, Mister Hawk?"

"Did you see the man at all?"

"No," Franklin Bosworth said. "I not only didn't see him, I had no warning he was close at all. One moment I was in my office in the back of the house. The next I was in bed with cold rags on my head." He made a grimacing smile. "Like riding a bucking horse, you understand. You reach for the saddle horn, and when you open your fingers, there's nothing but grass in them. That quick."

"I see." John looked at the older son. "You looked for tracks?"

A nod but no words.

John put out his cigarette leisurely. "Listen, Mister Bosworth," he said to the son. "I didn't rob your father. I know nothing about it at all. But I have a damned good reason to want to see the man caught. I'll explain that later. If you saw any tracks, will you tell me what they were like?"

The son looked at John for a long time before he spoke. "Mister Hawk," he said in a strong, deep voice, "my brother and father and I have a little secret between us about that man. If they're willing to share it with you . . . after what you've told us about our horses . . . then I'll tell you. Otherwise, no."

John felt sweat on his forehead. He looked at the older man, saw that he was being subjected to a close and intent scrutiny. "Well, sir?" he said.

The older man looked around at his sons. Neither looked anything but formidable. He sighed. "Go ahead, Tom. Tell him."

But Tom said: "What do you think, Herb?"

The younger man at the door was frowning. "I don't know. He's told us he's an outlaw."

"Pshaw," their father said. "It was my head, boys. Besides, after sixty years of running from, and after, men, I think I can read a man fair-to-middling well. Go on, Tom."

Tom said: "There were horse tracks, Mister Hawk. Horse and boot tracks."

"Odd markings?"

Tom shook his head thoughtfully, eyes bright and shiny. "Not especially odd, but both were worn enough so's we'd know them again."

John frowned. "Is that all?"

"No," their father said impatiently. "There was a scratched place on the pantry doorway, Mister Hawk, gun high. It was on the left side of the door jamb."

"Left side?"

Tom nodded, and stood up from his chair. "The left side," he repeated after his father. "Left side and as high as I wear my gun."

"I see." John drew up a chair finally and sank down into it. There was one man whose gun he recalled as being worn on the left side and whose height would correspond with Tom Bosworth's height. It made his heart beat strongly. After a moment he said: "Well, you've probably noticed my gun's on the right side." Only one head nodded, Franklin Bosworth's. The sons remained unmoved and unmoving. "I reckon the size would be about right though, wouldn't it?"

"Close enough," the youngest son said shortly.

John gazed at him, saw a youth's quickness of perception and quickness to rush headlong into error. He nodded at the younger man. "The man's tracks," he said. "Were they about like mine would be?"

It was Tom who answered. "No, that's what influenced me to tell you what we know about the man. He wouldn't be as heavy as you are. The tracks were shallower than you'd make, even on dry ground."

"Well, that's something," John said, admittedly feeling better.

Franklin Bosworth said: "Exactly what've you got on your mind, Mister Hawk?"

"This. I believe I know who robbed you. I think I know why it was done, aside from the money, of course. And I'm going to ask the three of you to listen to me for a moment."

He told them what he thought Jameson was trying to do. They listened stoically, all but the father, and his pleasant, big face became steadily craggier and craggier until John was finished, then he leaned forward in his chair.

"Mister Hawk, I don't suppose you know that Smalley and Curt Jameson are tolerably well known hereabouts. They've been in these parts quite a number of years. Now I'm going to tell you that those two are scoundrels and I know they are."

John looked wry. "I'm finding it out, but what I'm hoping the three of you'll do is keep what you know about your robber to yourselves. Then, when I'm arrested for the crime as I've just told you I expect to be, you'll come out in the open and prove that I couldn't have done it."

Tom said: "You said you knew who the robber was."

"Well, I know him by sight, not by name."

"Then describe him."

But John demurred. "Not yet. Not until the lid's ready to blow off. Then you can have him, Mister Bosworth."

Now the father scowled, and it completely altered his face, lent it an air of thunderous quality. "No," he said, "I can't hold for that, Mister Hawk." His deep voice was hard and uncompromising. "We want that man. If he's allowed to run loose, he might attack someone else."

"Or leave the country," the younger son said with asperity. "Describe him, Hawk."

John leaned back in the chair. "Sorry," he said. "I've got a lot to lose in this. Maybe my life, and since my stake's biggest, I want it my way."

Tom Bosworth moved across the room, surprisingly light and quiet for his bulk. He stopped beside his father's chair. There was a hard flintiness to his eyes, but they were inflamed with the willingness to gamble, more than to command. "And if your figuring is right," he said, "Jeff Smalley's law will be after you very shortly."

"I believe so."

"Then," he said harshly, "I think my father and brother and I will hang around a spell and see what happens."

John reflected, thinking that half friends under the circumstances were better than no friends at all. He nodded. "As you wish."

So the shadows lengthened slightly as the sun slid off the meridian and the office was treated to desultory conversation in which, over a long period of time, John told the three Bosworths his story, omitting what he thought was neither pertinent nor important. Into this category fell Jack Keeney's background and his acquaintanceship with Joyce Porter. They listened and relaxed and eventually Tom Bosworth elaborated on their suspicions concerning the man who had robbed them.

Then Cleve returned and his eyes were troubled. John motioned him farther into the room, introduced him.

"What's on your mind, Cleve?"

"There's a rumor, John. . . ."

John's lips quirked a little. "What is it?"

"The boy heard it. . . . Charley, our greaser."

"Well?"

"That the sheriff is looking for you, John." Agitation came up forcibly into Cleve's face.

"Must not be looking very hard," John said dryly. "I've been here all afternoon. What's rumor say I'm wanted for?"

"Armed robbery, John."

"All right," John said calmly. "If I'm taken in, you run the place until I'm back and see that Jack Keeney is told. Understand?"

"I'll do my best, John."

CHAPTER SIX

Looking at Cleve, Tom Bosworth said: "Where did you hear this?"

"Uh . . . the lad who greases our coaches was over at Jameson's livery barn. He heard it over there."

Franklin Bosworth straightened in his chair. "Strikes me odd," he said, "a rumor like that would be circulating *before* the law starts to move."

John said: "Unless someone at the barn overheard the arrest planned before it was taken to the law."

"Well," Tom Bosworth said, rising, "however it happened, I think Herb'd best go hurry Eb up, Dad."

His father looked around. "Why? Eb'll make it in good time."

"Not now he won't," Tom said. "Jeff Smalley moves fast once he starts moving. The three of us'd have to back down against big odds like Smalley'll bring, if there's trouble."

Franklin Bosworth's head hung low a moment, then he moved it sideways toward the boy by the door. "Go ahead, Herb. Tom's right."

The younger man wheeled out the door, climbed into his father's rig, turned it, and flicked the lines.

Tom Bosworth was looking at John. "If anything went wrong, Hawk," he said, "you'd be the only one who knows the man we want."

John got out of his chair, crossed to Cleve's desk, sat down, and began to write. The office was silent except for the scratching of pencil upon paper. When he finished, he jerked his head toward Cleve who still hung fearfully in the outer doorway. When Cleve approached, John said: "Send the greaser to Jack with this. Have him deliver it personally."

"Now?"

"Right now. You stay out there and see him off."

Cleve folded the paper as he hurried from the room. John went back around the counter, leaned upon it, looking at the younger Bosworth. "The man's description is in that note," he said. "If anything happens to me, my partner'll identify him to you. All right?"

"What's the mystery?"

"No mystery," John said. "I just don't want anyone to jump the gun. That man may be handier alive than dead, at least as far as getting Smalley and Jameson is concerned."

He had no sooner stopped speaking than Curt Jameson swung through the outer door, stopped in obvious surprise, and nodded at the Bosworths. "Well," he said, "good afternoon."

Tom Bosworth remained silent and unmoving, regarding the big liveryman stonily. Franklin Bosworth nodded gravely at Jameson, who plunged a hand into a coat pocket and brought forth a cigar, bit off its end, and lit it before advancing farther into the room.

"John, I'd like a word with you."

"Shoot," John said.

Jameson's eyes narrowed the smallest bit. "Privately," he added.

John pushed off the counter and led the way to the door leading into the stable yard. Jameson followed him. When they were out where the slanting rays of the sun gave back an eye-stinging brilliance off the bare ground, Jameson stopped. His face had settled into an expression of coldness.

"I've had a buyer out after hay, John. It seems like you've

also had a buyer out."

"I have."

"And all I got was one ton."

John leaned against the back wall of the office. "Is that so?" he said disinterestedly.

"You don't need as much as you've bought, John."

"I think I will," John said.

Jameson's eyes showed antagonism, scarcely controlled. "Will you sell me ten ton?" he asked.

"Afraid not."

The antagonism flared out openly. "Why not?"

"I just told you. I might need it all."

"That's foolish. You couldn't put out ten tons of feed all winter long, let alone as much as you've bought."

"You said," John spoke out firmly, "I was to run this stage line like it belonged to me. Without any interference from you. That's exactly how I'm running it, and I was raised to believe that too much hay is just barely enough."

"But," Jameson said in outraged protest, "there isn't a chance of you feeding all the hay you've bought in five years."

"I've bought it and I intend to keep it."

"I know what you paid for it. I'll give you five dollars a ton profit and have it hauled, myself."

"The answer is still no!"

Jameson's cigar grew rigid, his voice rose a little, became unpleasantly shrill and roiled. "Listen, John, I think I know why you bought all the hay in the country. It was to force me to pay you a big profit."

John shook his head. "You're dead wrong. I had no intention of selling any hay at all."

"Oh. You're forcing me to import hay, is that it?"

"That's your business, not mine."

"In other words," Jameson said sharply, "you're looking for

trouble with me."

John came off the wall. "Listen, Jameson," he said. "I wasn't originally looking for trouble with you or anyone else, but lately it's begun to look to me like you and your partner, Smalley, are out for trouble with me. If that's the case, I'm here to oblige."

Jameson's face blossomed a dark, splotchy red. "And you had a hand in wrecking my new stage, too, didn't you?"

John was surprised. "I don't know what you're talking about," he said.

"Don't you? You didn't know someone put steel filings in the grease of all four wheels and after fifteen miles both axles were so chewed up my man had to abandon the coach on the road to Vacaville, did you?"

"No, I didn't know that," John said, remembering Jack Keeney's enigmatic attitude when they'd discussed Jameson's new coach, knowing for certain who had ruined the coach, and totally astonished by his secret knowledge. "What did you need a new coach for, anyway, since you're out of the stage business?"

"You'll find out," Jameson said, half turning toward the door. "You're going to find out a lot of things now that you want to fight me."

John reached for Jameson's coat, tugged sharply. "Maybe the same man put filings in your grease, who tried to do just that right here a few nights back. Why don't you ask him, Jameson?"

"What are you talking about, Hawk? You must be out of your mind. Let go. . . ."

"Maybe I'm out of my mind about some rumors you and your partner've started, too. And about the Smalley and Jameson Stage and Cartage Company. And about a lot of other underhanded things you've been doing. Even about why you were so tickled when I paid off the promissory note. Instead of stealing six hundred dollars by ruining my reputation, running me out of business, now you stand to get rid of me, get the line back, and keep the five thousand as well."

Jameson was pale. "You've been drinking," he said.

"I don't drink, just an occasional ale. That's not it by a damned sight. You're as crooked as a dog's hind leg, Jameson. It's not me who's been hunting trouble, it's you, and the way you've been doing it is about as underhanded as a man can be."

"And you've been crying to old Bosworth," Jameson said.

"I'm the man who robbed him, remember? Smalley's law'll be coming for me. Well, you and Smalley've got a cougar by the tail this time. You want a fight and you're sure going to get one. I'll make you earn every damned dime of that five thousand, believe me."

"This is crazy," Jameson said, badly shaken. "I don't know what half of this means."

"The only thing you don't know," John said, "is that you've overplayed your hand right down the line. Smalley'll like that. They tell me he's shrewd. If he is, he'll be madder'n a boiled owl over your stupidity. Go on back and tell him you're a horse's rear-end, then don't forget to show up at the contract bidding with your new Red River coach. I'll probably be there, and if I am, I aim to tell the government people how good your equipment is and what kind of a fellow you are. Now go on and tell Smalley . . . if you've got the guts. Get out of here and stay out. The next time you come through the front door, come loaded. Now move."

And John propelled Jameson through the rear door, stood in its opening, watching the heavy body cross the room without looking at the Bosworths, and disappear beyond, out where the roadway was flat and hot under the wavering sunlight.

Tom Bosworth broke the stillness. He said: "You talk kind of loud when you're mad."

The elder Bosworth had moved his chair a little so as to see the entire room. He watched John close the back door, cross to a chair, and drop down into it. "Now," he said tartly, "the cat's out of the bag."

"I said more than I should have, all right," John admitted.

"Doesn't make much difference," Tom Bosworth said. "I don't know about *all* of it, but one thing you said sure is true . . . Jeff Smalley'll be plenty put out when he hears you know as much as you told Jameson. Jeff sort of likes to keep things quiet until the last moment. When he catches a man off guard, he lets him have both barrels." Tom inclined his head. "Its worked real well, too, that system of his."

Franklin Bosworth was leaning forward a little, gazing at John. "Mister Hawk," he, said softly, "is this stage line your only purpose for staying in Vacaville?"

"No, not my only purpose."

"If you'll excuse an old man," Bosworth said, "exactly what else is on your mind?"

John looked up. "Why do you ask?"

"Well, it's like this. Now and then I invest in what I consider foolproof enterprises. You see, if you intended to stay in Vacaville. . . ."

"I intend to stay all right," John said, "but I'm not sure you'd call this a foolproof enterprise. Maybe just the opposite. Anyway, I don't need money as far as the line's concerned."

"No," Bosworth said, "I didn't mean you, particularly. I was wondering if you'd have any objection to my acquiring Jameson's half interest."

"No," John said slowly, "I suppose not, providing the terms were satisfactory."

"Oh, that," Bosworth said, leaning back. "You could make the terms yourself."

And John, gazing at the older man, had an idea. Arising, he

said: "I wonder if you'd come out in the yard with me for a moment?"

Franklin Bosworth got out of his chair, nodding. "Lead the way," he said.

Tom watched them until the door closed, then turned his head at the approaching sound of two sets of footfalls.

Outside a light breeze was hurrying past overhead. A sound of tree leaves rubbing together came and went. "You asked about my other plans," John said to Bosworth. "I'll tell you about them. I'm here for just one reason . . . to make good. I've been a cowboy all my life, a drifter. I stole your horses to get enough money to buy into a business." He reached over and knuckled the office's back wall. "This business. All the rest that's happened has come out of a hope that I could make good. But that's not all. I want to marry Judge Porter's daughter. . . ." He paused, seeking surprise in the other man's face, only there was none to see. "So, in a few words, that's it."

"Yes," Franklin Bosworth said, "I knew about the last part of it."

"You knew?"

The big man nodded. "Mister Hawk, Joyce Porter has been like a daughter to our family for the past twenty years. Now then, normally I'm not a questioning man, never have been, you see, because when I was younger we considered it rude to ask questions." The imperturbable gray eyes sparkled. "Also, sometimes it could be unhealthy. But when Joyce came riding up *before* breakfast, mind you, all of us knew something was wrong this morning. Now let me say that my wife and Tom's wife, being women, had the whole story before I'd hardly finished with the outside chores. Of course they told me."

"The whole story?" John said.

"Yes, even about our horses. That should make it easier for you to understand why my youngest boy, Herb, stood by the door when we all came in, and why Tom went over by the wall, on your right. I've another son, Eben . . . we call him Eb . . . well, sir, he was to round up our riders and some of the closest neighbors and drift into town later . . . just in case, you see."

"Oh."

"But where you're concerned, I believe we're all satisfied now, Mister Hawk."

"Well. . . ."

"And another thing. Joyce wouldn't want her father told about the horses, I don't imagine."

"No."

"But I expect you'd like him to have a good regard for you . . . ?"

"Yes, I would."

"But you'll agree that right now wouldn't be a good time to approach him . . . ?"

"I suppose not," John said, just as the rear door swung wide and Tom Bosworth's frame filled the opening.

"The law's here."

John reëntered the room behind Franklin Bosworth. The man he faced was four inches taller than any other man in the room and he weighed less, as well. He was thin to the point of emaciation.

"Are you John Hawk?"

"I am."

"I have a warrant for your arrest."

"On what charge?"

"Armed robbery."

Tom Bosworth cleared his throat; otherwise there wasn't a sound. The sheriff had a big-boned deputy with him, fleshy and ineffably soft-looking, coarse of feature with eyes too widely apart and a pendulous jaw eloquent of animal courage and limited intelligence. The deputy was sucking on a frayed match in silence by the doorway.

"Who did I rob?"

The sheriff colored and his eyes moved to Franklin Bosworth with uncertainty. "This man here," he said. "Franklin Bosworth."

And Tom Bosworth made a barking little laugh and said: "Just like a pattern, isn't it?"

Behind the deputy John saw Cleve materialize in the opening of the doorway. The clerk's face was dappled with agitation and perspiration.

"All right," John said finally. "I'm ready." He nodded toward the Bosworths.

The sheriff stepped aside. His dull deputy's countenance brightened a little as John walked past toward the plank walk. Without a backward glance both lawmen followed John.

They took him to a small building that had *Sheriff* painted across it in bold black letters, and led him inside. The deputy took his six-gun, felt for other weapons, and moved around front, tossed the gun upon a scarred desk, and perched on one corner of the desk, and began swinging a leg indolently.

The sheriff avoided John's gaze. "Put what's in your pockets here," he said, indicating the desk top. "That's fine, now give me your name, age, address and occupation." He wrote in a crabbed hand, letters unevenly round and stilted-looking. Threw the pencil down and stood up. "Come on."

After he was locked in the deep, narrow metal cage, John asked who had sworn out the warrant. The sheriff looked at him stonily for a moment. "In this territory," he said, "we don't need anything but the knowledge that a crime's been committed to arrest a culprit."

John smiled thinly. "I hope your court needs more than that," he said, "before it sentences." The sheriff turned away.

There was an unclean odor to the cell-block. It was partitioned from the front office by an incredibly thick adobe wall. John surmised at least half the sheriff's quarters had once been part of a much older building left over from the days when Mexico ruled the Southwest.

He sat down on the straw-filled sack that served as mattress to the wall bunk, and created a cigarette. Blue smoke hung in the air undisturbed by freshets. Its scent was pleasant. He removed his hat, leaned back across the bunk until his back touched the wall. Overhead was a long, narrow, barred window, a mere slit in the mud wall.

He thought he'd guessed wrong. Jameson, he'd opined, in spite of how it might make him appear in his partner's eyes, would go directly to Smalley. And Smalley, hearing how much John knew, would have stopped the preconceived plan to arrest him. Especially after Jameson told him about the Bosworths. It hadn't worked out that way.

He inhaled, exhaled, watched the smoke go up, falter, then hang motionlessly. It hadn't worked that way because Jameson hadn't gone to Smalley. Hadn't gone obviously, because of fear. Fear and the certainty that he'd look stupid in Smalley's eyes as soon as Smalley heard that John hadn't bested Jameson once, but twice. Closed Jameson out of the local hay market and ruined his Red River coach as well.

The latter thought made John remember. Now, thinking back, he wondered at the blindness that had kept him from surmising Jack had something like steel filings on his mind. The way he'd walked from the office without saying anything. The far-away look when he'd been atop the box with Ford Tull that same evening. Well, it was done, and whatever he thought now was beside the point. Of course, the ruined stage was a blessing. A lot might be thought and said now and later but nothing would alter the fact that without equipment Jameson's new company would get no mail contract. Did Smalley know? Apparently,

John thought, he didn't. That amused him.

Shadows lengthened, drew out along the wall, softened a host of scratched initials and names, crude art work and obscenities. They brought with them a vague chill that never went beyond its initial coolness. Flat shadows that were peculiar to jails. Neither round nor fragrant like shadows outside a jail. Never warm or pleasant, simply heralding an end to something called a day that every jail was filled with endlessly.

Jeff Smalley came, after the deputy had lit the solitary lamp in the dingy corridor beyond John's doorway. Smalley with his head set squarely on sloping shoulders and a phantom shadow, tall and lanky, following after him, stopping when Smalley stopped, peering with the eyes of a killer through the gloom at John, smiling.

"Well, Hawk," the saloon man said banteringly, "you never can tell who you'll see in one of these places."

John still smoked. Now he took a long inhalation and blew it upward, watched it, didn't look around.

"Pretty calm about it," Smalley said. Then he laughed a short, bursting laugh, unamused and hard-sounding. "Too bad. Y'know, when a man breaks the law in this country, he usually don't hang around, or, if he does, he heads for the Running Horse. Our customers aren't molested and we got nice crap tables."

Then John's head came around slowly. Through the shadows he studied Smalley's face and said: "I reckon that means when a man's outside the law here he ought to know better'n go it alone in the Vacaville country."

Smalley's eyes were dark and still. He didn't pursue John's remark. "Another thing to remember, Hawk . . . when you're in a new country, find out whose toes *not* to step on."

"Next time I'll find that out first," John said, and put out his cigarette.

"You think there'll be a next time?"

"I think so, yes."

"How come you're so sure?"

John's glance was upon the tied-down left-hand gun on the grinning phantom's thigh when he answered. "Because, whether I robbed Bosworth or not . . . and you'll know about *that* . . . the crime's not one you can hang a man for."

"But how about horse stealing?" Smalley asked genially. Because of the darkness where John sat, he failed to see the sudden rigidity, the withheld breath. "There's been a lot of that around the country, too, Hawk. I got a notion if some of the folks who've lost animals were to come in here there might be an identification or two."

John resumed breathing; the freezing fear drained away slowly, the terrible sinking sensation. A shot in the dark but a perilously frightening one. He moved on the bunk, extended his legs, crossed them, and gazed at his boots. "I have no way of knowing exactly what you're after," he told Smalley, "but I don't think it's a hanging."

"What do you think it is, then?"

"Money, maybe." He looked up, fastened his eyes to Smalley's dim face. "Half of the five thousand Curt Jameson got from me."

"How'd you arrive at that?"

"If you're his partner, you'd expect to get half of it. You'd expect him to split with you after I'm out of the way."

Smalley went closer to the cell, put a hand up, and grasped the cold steel with it. "After you're out of the way? Why'd you say that?"

John kept his thoughts secret, drifted with the conversation. "I'm in here for an armed robbery I didn't commit. You know it and I know it."

"And?"

"But somebody's after my hide. As I've figured it out, it's you and Jameson. If I'm sent to prison, Jameson takes back his stage line on default. I lose five thousand dollars. You and Jameson split it. Works out pretty clever, I'd say."

"That's the way you've got it figured, is it?" Smalley said. "Well, if it's true . . . if you go to prison . . . how long do you think you'll get for armed robbery?"

John shrugged. "That'd be up to the law that put me in here, wouldn't it?"

"It sure would," Smalley said swiftly, "and Vacaville law doesn't like assault trials. You could get a long stretch. A real long stretch." Then Smalley bent closer. "But I think you'd rather head for Mexico for a year or two myself. I might be wrong though, Hawk."

"No, you wouldn't be," John said from back in the gloom. "Not by a damned sight you wouldn't."

Smalley straightened up, glanced over his shoulder at his bodyguard. "Fetch me a pencil from the sheriff's office, will you?"

After the slow-moving Texan had gone, Smalley jerked his head at John. "Come over here closer." John went and the shorter man's face was markedly intent in the musty light. "All right, Hawk, you've got the idea. There'll be a horse just outside that little window up near the top of your cell, come dawn tomorrow. A saddled horse, d'you understand?"

"What about the bars over that little window?"

"You can take them out with your bare hands. When you get on that horse, Hawk, don't look back. Hit the trail south and keep going."

John began to shake his head. "If the horse'll be there . . . who else will with a shotgun?"

"Nothing like that," Smalley said quickly. "You get on and ride off, free and safe. There's just one thing you'd better never forget. Don't ever come back to the Vacaville country."

John made a bitter laugh. "Is five thousand dollars what I pay for getting clear?"

"That's right," Smalley said bluntly. "You've bought your neck clear of a hang rope. But if we ever hear that you're back in the country, believe me, Hawk, you'll never get closer'n carbine range. Keep that in the back of your head."

"So you and Jameson got twelve thousand dollars out of this, didn't you?"

Smalley nodded without any hesitancy. "Sure. Bosworth's money and yours. If that makes you feel bad, cry while you're riding, and if you don't ride, I can promise you a hang rope."

"I'll ride, all right," John said, and knew his words were the same ones at least two other men had uttered under identical circumstances. "But you're not so sure of your case you'd risk fetching me before a court, are you?"

"Court, hell," Smalley said sharply. "Where'd you get that court idea? Your kind's tried out at the edge of town where there's an old oak tree. There wouldn't be any court trial at all."

John half turned away. "All right," he said. "Don't forget, Smalley, no gun behind me when I ride out of town because I might live through it and hunt you up." He returned to the bunk against the wall and ignored the left-handed deputy when he returned and made a show of handing Jeff Smalley a pencil.

When the sounds of the town came, later, there was a new loneliness in them. Muted by the wall, softened by distance, he heard them all, and when the unintelligent deputy brought him food on a tin plate, he ignored him.

"Better eat," the deputy said, and left the food upon the floor just inside the door, went back up the corridor with his footfalls making loud, hollow echoes.

There was no surprise in finding his predicament exactly as he'd thought it would be. There was no special cause for fear, either, except insofar as he'd tilted his hand to Curt Jameson. He thought about it until the noises beyond the jail died away one at a time and Vacaville became silent beneath a jeweled sky.

By now the Bosworths would have evolved a plan of action. By now, too, Joyce would know. And that brought up a doubt that had lingered briefly during his conversation with Smalley. But since Smalley's plans were for John to escape, he considered it highly improbable that Judge Porter was part of the crooked combine that ruled Vacaville.

Thinking back, John was disinclined to wonder. Besides the judge's open face, clear gaze, there was the very unwillingness on Smalley's part to bring formal charges.

And Jack . . . ? He would know by now, at least, that their enemies were out in the open. In the back of Jack's mind would lie the exact knowledge John didn't have—Keeney's association with Jeff Smalley and how it could be used to hurt Jack. If, as Jack had said, Smalley could put the law on him, the wisest course for Jack would be to make tracks. And yet, in his own note to Jack, all he'd said was that trouble was coming. Now it was here and Jack didn't know it. There was dread in that, but John didn't dwell upon it beyond noting that the first person he saw who he could trust, he'd send down to Springerville with the warning to his partner.

And Joyce . . . ?

He turned away from that vision, too.

The Bosworths. Strangely, the ones he'd hurt the most, and knew the least, were the ones he felt the most dependence upon. What were they all doing?

He moved on the bunk, made himself more comfortable against the wall. Whatever it was, he himself had to accept Jeff Smalley's bounty so far as escape and the saddled horse were concerned. After that he must, first, warn Jack, see that he got away before Smalley heard about him and sent a killer after him, or vented his antagonism by acquainting some lawman with Keeney's whereabouts.

He thought, and without being aware that he was tired, he was, and without knowing when, he fell asleep, propped against the wall, sitting upon the straw mattress. And when he awakened there was a sound beyond his cell. A steady thumping of something like a gun butt against the wall.

It took a moment for him to remember, another moment for him to limber aching legs and stand up. Overhead the tiny window looked too small for his body. He took a nail keg that served as the cell's solitary piece of furniture, placed it below the high opening, and strained upward. With effort he could reach the bars. Each one came away noiselessly in his hand. They weren't mortised in at all, just placed upright and wedged a little.

The noise along the outer wall ceased. He put each bar upon the floor where they'd be easy to locate, and smiled when he did it. No point in causing so obliging a sheriff the inconvenience of having to make new bars.

He drew himself to the flange of the little ledge, forced his shoulders through the opening, and peered down. The horse was there, saddled and bridled and endlessly patient. The same horse and saddle he'd originally ridden into Vacaville. Beyond the horse there wasn't anything that looked out of place, unusual, but that meant nothing for nearby buildings, dark, hushed, sightless, could conceal a sniper or an army of snipers. He wondered, balancing there, if Curt Jameson had screwed his nerve up enough to tell Smalley what John had said to him, decided he hadn't, for with John gone there would be no other witness to Jameson's errors.

He wiggled a little farther out, guessed the drop to be about twelve feet, regretted the necessity to go headfirst, and hoped he'd be able to bend his body, roll, or perhaps get his hands out to break the fall before he struck the ground.

As it turned out, though, his body turned completely over in its fall. He landed on his feet, staggered an instant, then straightened up and went across to the horse, received a dispassionate regard, and swung up. A dog began barking close by as he reined around and felt a tremor pass across his shoulders as he booted the beast out. No bullet came.

Starlight made a pale carpet for him to ride upon, going south. He kept the horse at a lope for half an hour, reined up suddenly to sit perfectly still, listening. There was nothing. No sound, no movement. He kneed the animal out again and left the softly lighted road, cut across the range a ways, then rode southward, parallel to it. He plodded at a long-legged walk for hours on end and, shortly before dawn, saw Springerville ahead.

He made a complete circle of the town before he left the horse in a chaparral clump, and went forward afoot. Several early riders went past, voices carrying with perfect clarity where John stood motionlessly waiting. After they'd passed, he went to the company's local corral and station. Finding the bunkhouse wasn't hard. Wondering who else might be in there—or if *anyone* might be there—he entered.

A long, bubbling series of breaths came out of the close blackness. He felt his way cautiously until he was above an occupied bunk. Bending low, he traced out the pinched-up, lean face. Rousing Jack wasn't hard. His eyes snapped open at the same instant his right hand darted beneath a folded jumper he employed as a pillow. John's grip closed over the wrist, forced it still.

"Hold it," he said. "It's me, John."

And Jack took a moment to make the adjustment, then he pushed himself upward and squinted. "Well," he said indefinitely.

"Did you get my note?"

"Sure, got it about ten tonight. Say, you're acting kind of funny. Anybody chasing you, John?"

John stood up straight. "I doubt it," he said. "They had me in jail, though."

Jack sat up straighter. "The hell they did!" he exclaimed. "I figured from the note hell was about to pop, only I didn't think it'd be right away. Hand me those pants, will you?" John pulled them off a nail and held them out. "Thanks. Now tell me what's happened."

John spoke hurriedly while Jack dressed, buckled on his gun, clamped a shapeless hat upon his head, ran his tongue around inside his mouth, and spat lustily. When John's voice finally died away, he said: "I expect we got a fight, haven't we?"

"You haven't."

"Huh?"

"Don't forget the law, Jack."

"Forget, hell," Keeney said irritably. "I'll *never* forget the law, but if we have to fight, I'll tell you *one* thing . . . when I go to hell, Jeff Smalley's going with me."

"No," John said, "you're out of this for now. There's something more important. You go back to Raton and make our bids on both those contracts when the date comes up. Bid them as low as Cleve's figures say we dare and still make a profit. The hell of that is that whoever bids for Smalley'll see you there."

Jack snorted. "They'll see me all right, and I hope it's Jeff himself. I'll make it a *point* that they see me."

John frowned. "I don't follow you. We want you to stay clear. . . ."

"Don't ever follow me. I'm touchy about folks following me. Just remember that Red River coach. Remember that, and that I'm down there for business and forget all the rest of it. What are *you* going to do? Go back up there and get those Bosworths?"

"If they're around," John said, "but first I want to see Judge Porter."

Jack began to shake his head. "Something I want to tell you," he said. "Jeff Smalley'll have you killed with no more thought than if you were a rattler. The thing to do as I see it is to go down to Raton with me and see the U.S. marshal. He could. . . ."

"And at the first scent of trouble we'd lose part of the men we want, too."

"Well, but you're. . . ."

"Come on, I'll help you saddle up. We've both got miles to go before sunup. By the way, did you hire another guard?"

"Yeah," Jack answered, feeling his way past dark objects. "I got us a regular rip-snorter. Spent yesterday teaching him how to run the station down here. I guess I'd better leave him a note." Emerging into the early chill, Jack sniffed the air while he felt in his pockets for pencil and paper. Abruptly he said: "Was Jameson put out over the coach?"

"He was fit to be tied."

"Well," Jack said, writing, "it serves him right for giving me the idea. I had to ride all night and most of the following day to get up there, fix his wagon, and get back down here." He held out the paper. "Here, I'll saddle up and you put this in the office on the desk."

John went to the office, then returned, untied his horse, let the reins lie in his hand until Jack rode up beside him. Then he mounted. "Get those bids," he said, "and keep that note with the description of Smalley's Texas gunman where it'll be safe. If anything happens to me, give it to the Bosworths."

"I understand. By the way, I know that squirt. His name's Chet Cantrell. Been Smalley's private gun for a couple of years now." Then Jack looked up with a widening gaze. "Say, are

119

those Bosworths the one . . . ones we . . . I . . . stole the horses from?"

"Yes."

Jack puckered up his face and wagged his head. "What a sweet mess *this* is," he reflected. "Well, John, don't turn your back on your best friend, and if you need me, send word. I'll set a record getting back."

John watched him disappear into the shading night, into a mantling duskiness that was paling imperceptibly, incredibly slowly, with the initial stirrings of dawn.

CHAPTER SEVEN

Franklin Bosworth smiled when he heard that John Hawk had escaped from the Vacaville jail. His three sons, three riders, and four closest neighbors were in the café, eating breakfast with him when the proprietor told of the escape.

It was said that John had worked the bars loose from a small window of his cell, made his escape that way. He had boldly gone to Jameson's livery barn and taken his own horse and saddle. The restaurant proprietor, like most of Vacaville, was outspoken in his conviction that Hawk was a resourceful, and probably dangerous, outlaw.

After Bosworth's men had eaten, they went out into the new day and clustered on the plank walk. Their numbers were noticeable because the town was only just stirring. Ten men standing together in conversation stood out. Curt Jameson, *en route* to his barn, saw them. A shaft of uneasiness swept upward in him. He went as far as the open maw of the barn and stood there, back a little, watching.

Tom Bosworth seemed to be carrying the main burden of the conversation. The neighboring cowmen sucked their teeth and listened. The Bosworth cowboys, weather-stained men all, struck from a similar pattern, lean, red-faced, clear-eyed, looked upon the town as they listened. Young Herb Bosworth and slightly older Eben Bosworth stood close behind their father. Their faces appeared intent.

Jameson wrestled with his fear and finally decided that Jeff

Smalley must be alerted. Accordingly he walked the full length of his barn and out the back passageway. Skirted around the slag and old iron littering the ground by Sean O'Brien's shoeing shop. Walked down the scruffy back alley until he was far enough south to risk crossing the main thoroughfare, and started past the last building.

The roadway was deserted both ways. Far north he could see that the little huddle of men had broken up. There were three men walking toward the stage company's office on the west side of the road. Beyond that there was no one visible. Jameson hesitated only long enough to notice this, then he started boldly across the road, got to the east side with his heart drumming rapidly in his ears, his fear a growing and unnerving thing. He went on down the side road as far as the alley that led north to the rear of Smalley's Running Horse Saloon, turned up it, and let a long uneven breath go past his lips. He walked with only the sound of his own steps as company, until he saw and recognized the mounds of refuse that lined both sides of the saloon's rear entrance. By then his fear had lessened considerably, enough so that a burning and savage hatred was coursing in him for the interfering Bosworths.

"Whoa there, Jameson."

He stopped. The fear returned with a rush, pushing out every other emotion, and made his face go cold in a stunned, set way.

The man who had stopped him was tall and angular with a bony face and a superficial, icy little smile. Both his thumbs were hooked into a dark shell belt. He leaned upon the off side of the farthest refuse pile near the saloon's back door.

"Goin' in for a drink? Whyn't you use the front door?"

The pale eyes teased, the long, thin mouth curved upward slightly. Jameson tried to remember the face and couldn't. "Who are you?" he said. "What do you want?"

"Me?" the bony face asked gently. "Why, I'm a Bosworth

rider is all." The long mouth waited, parted. "What I want is you. Mister Bosworth's over in your office at the barn, Jameson. He wants to talk to you."

"Well, I don't want to talk to him. Now get out of my way."

Then the cowboy's smile grew genuinely amused. "I'm not in your way," he said, and stood away from the refuse pile, loosely, thin and appearing mild. "But you'd best come along and see the boss."

"I'll see Bosworth when I damned well feel like it," Jameson said. He forced his legs to work, rise and fall in a mechanical, mincing way as he started up the narrow path toward the doorway.

"You'll feel like it," the cowboy said, some of his humor getting an edge, "right now."

And Jameson stopped again. "I've got something else to do first," he said.

"Naw, you'd better do whatever that is later. Now come on."

And Jameson went. Whisked away from help when he could have almost reached out and touched it.

The loose-jointed rider shuffled along behind him, wearing the amused little grin again, watching the heavier man's body quiver when he walked.

Inside the livery barn were Eb and Herb Bosworth and three men Curt Jameson recognized as hill ranchers, neighbors of the Bosworths. They stood in silence, watching him enter. None nodded, none spoke. He knew the younger Bosworth as a volatile, blunt man, so when Herb jerked his head toward the office door, Jameson went in.

Franklin Bosworth looked up at him from Jameson's own desk. He looked deceptively affable. The ice-blue eyes, in their craggy setting with fine hair lines going outward across the seamed face, were even radiating a warmth.

" 'Morning, Curt. Sit down."

Jameson sat, hunched over, and closed one fist around the other one.

"We've been waiting for you," Bosworth said easily. "Tom's up at the stage office." The old face assumed an apologetic look. "Sorry if we had to interrupt anything."

Jameson cleared his throat, said nothing.

"It's about the stage line, Curt. I expect now that your ex-partner's turned out to be an outlaw, you'll be taking it over again." Bosworth's eyebrows went up but Jameson still said nothing.

"That's usually the way, isn't it, when a partner defaults?"

Jameson moved on the chair. "Why?" he said finally. "What's this all about?"

"I'll get right to the point," Bosworth said, his voice going flatter, becoming more brisk. "I'd like to buy you out of the line."

Jameson's eyes widened a trifle. "Buy *me* out?"

"Yes."

"No," Jameson said quickly. "It's not for sale. I mean, the stage line's not for sale."

Bosworth gazed at Jameson unblinkingly, then he shrugged. "All right," he said, "if that's the way you want it, but I thought you'd rather either own it outright or have your partner own it outright. Partnerships with some men aren't too successful."

"I'm not worried about that," Jameson said.

"If you think you and I can get along, it suits me."

Jameson frowned. "Why should I think about that?" he asked.

Bosworth looked mildly astonished. "Haven't you heard, Curt? You and I are partners in the company. I bought out John Hawk yesterday."

"What!"

"Sure, I thought you'd have heard. . . . Well, on second thought, maybe you wouldn't have heard it after all. They took him away pretty quick."

Jameson was stunned.

Bosworth turned, took his hat off Jameson's desk, put it on, prepared to rise. "I just thought maybe you'd rather have me buy you out altogether, you see. Either that or you'd buy me out." He got up heavily. "Because, for one thing, Curt, I'm against the company taking mail and bullion contracts, and I know you're not. My past experiences have made me think small lines like ours ought to just haul passengers." He patted his coat where it bulged over a gun. "In other words, I believe we'd have friction right from the start, you see, and I'd rather live in peace with my friends."

Jameson gazed up at the old man for a moment, then he also arose. "I don't believe you bought Hawk out. He never told me. . . ."

"No law says he has to, Curt. Well, I got. . . ."

"You're lying."

Franklin Bosworth looked steadily into the red face. "You know," he said, "that's a poor thing to say to a man when you're unarmed, Curt."

"Prove you bought him out," Jameson said.

Bosworth patted his coat. "I've got the papers right here. Haven't had time to record them, but I intend to as soon as the lawyer shows up for business. Now, about that lying business. . . ."

Jameson reached for the door, wrenched it open, and flung himself through it. Tom Bosworth was approaching with his brother Eb. He reached out easily and caught Jameson, held him squirming at arm's length. Saliva showed on Jameson's mouth. Tom looked to the office doorway where his father stood, watching in a detached way.

"You want him?" Tom asked.

The elder Bosworth shook his head. "Let him go, Tom."

Jameson fled with six pairs of somber eyes upon him. He went directly across the road, kicking up little puddles of dust. He threw himself at the Running Horse's louvered doors and hauled up inside the bare room. Two men turned and gazed at him, a barkeeper and Jeff Smalley, freshly shaved and dressed but still sleep-puffy-looking.

"Well," Smalley said dryly, "what in hell stung you?"

"Come in here," Jameson said sharply, and headed for the empty gambling room.

Smalley looked at his bartender, shrugged, and went after Jameson, listened to the tumbling, breathless revelation with cold eyes, stuck a cigar between his teeth, lit it, and blew the smoke upward.

"So the old buzzard's taking Hawk's side, is he? Well, let him, for all the good it'll do him."

"But, dammit, Jeff, if he bucks us on the contracts. . . ."

"He won't buck anyone," Jeff Smalley said bleakly. "First off, I think he's a damned liar. I don't believe that yarn about Hawk selling out to him. In the second place, even if Hawk did sell to him, it wasn't a legal sale. Hawk was an outlaw at the time Bosworth said he bought him out. I'll get the lawyer to make a case on that."

"We. . . ."

"Shut up!" Smalley smoked in silence a moment. "All right, Bosworth's buying into this. I'll make him wish to God he'd never seen Hawk at all."

"His sons are with him and some of those hill ranchers from up. . . ."

"Curt," Smalley interrupted coldly, "is there something going on I don't know about?"

Jameson paled. "What do you mean?"

"That's what I'm asking, damn it. When I talked to Hawk, he acted like the others . . . scairt, suspicious, but ready to pull out

126

and stay out. But why would Bosworth be in this so strong unless he and Hawk'd talked a lot? Unless Bosworth knows something I don't know."

"Well," Jameson said, "Hawk went out and bought all the hay around Vacaville. Froze me out of the local sources."

Smalley gazed steadily at Jameson for a moment, then he smiled at him. "He did, did he? Why?"

"To keep me from getting hay, I reckon."

Smalley's smile deepened. "He was that smart? Hell, I guessed him just another horse rider. I'll be damned. Why would he be after you?"

Jameson shrugged, mumbled something unintelligible.

Smalley, watching him, nodded. "So's he could make you pay through the nose, then use your own money to get you out of the stage line. I'll be dogged, Jameson, we underestimated that feller."

"I'm not worrying about *him*. . . ."

"No, I'm not, either. And I'm not worrying about Bosworth."

"I am."

"Sure," Smalley said. "You would. Leave Bosworth to me. I'll skin him and nail his hide to the wall."

"He's got at least ten men with him, Jeff."

Jeff gestured contemptuously with his cigar. "I've got a few handy fellers of my own, but I don't think it'll come to that. We'll wait a little, until the lawyer gets to his office, then I'll go hire him to represent us. First off, he's to see if Bosworth records any bill of sale from Hawk. If he does, then we'll make a case of it. If he doesn't . . ."—Smalley put the cigar back into his mouth, bit down upon it.—"if he doesn't, you're sole owner of the line . . . on paper, anyway. We'll file default papers against Hawk like you did with those other fellers, and file notices of exclusive ownership again. Hawk'll be out in the cold, you'll have the line back, and we split five thousand dollars. Understand?"

Jameson's color had come back as Smalley talked. Now he straightened up and nodded. "All right. But those Bosworths look like they're going to stick around town today. I don't like running into them."

Smalley made a scornful sound. "Go hide in your office," he said, and turned away.

Curt Jameson went tentatively to the doorway of the Running Horse, stood just beyond the opening where the thin shade lay. Across the road his livery barn looked deserted although suspicion peopled it, in his mind anyway, with the same stony-faced crew who had been there before. He hesitated, then moved down to the plank walk. The morning was sparkling clear. The sun's brightness was intensely transparent. Distance was dissolved, abridged; mountains seemed to have come closer. Fall was in the air with a crispness.

He looked up and down the plank walks on both sides of the road. There were people out now, rigs moving in and out of town, merchants sweeping off the walkways. Southward his eyes hung upon two people deep in talk. One was Tom Bosworth, the other was that Porter girl. Jameson watched them a moment then, when the traffic was thickest, hurried across the roadway and disappeared into the perpetually damp and gloomy interior of his livery barn

Tom Bosworth had seen the scuttling figure, watched it twist through the traffic, and missed some of what Joyce was saying.

". . . not to Mexico, Tom." There was protest in her tone.

Tom looked down again. "I suppose not," he said. "But who knows? Men react differently, Joyce."

"You don't know *him*."

"No," Tom agreed, "I don't. Anyway, I'm half of a notion like you say. I expect he's around somewhere. The thing is . . . where?"

"Didn't any of you go see him when he was in jail?"

"No," Tom said. "We thought it'd be a bad thing to do. It wasn't very bright of us to hang around, as it was. Of course, you never know what's exactly the right thing to do at a time like that, but Paw said to stay away from the jail. He said Hawk did enough when he got mad at Jameson. That if Jeff found out how much Hawk and the rest of us knew. . . ."

"I understand," she said. She twisted a little, gazed up the roadway with swiftly moving, probing eyes. "Will they believe what your father told them about buying the stage line?"

Tom followed her gaze with a piercingly inquiring look of his own. "Darned if I know, Joyce," he said. "Paw just thought of it after breakfast. But I can tell you one thing. It scared the dickens out of Jameson. You should have seen his face."

"What did he do?"

"Went over to see Smalley in a lope. By now Jeff ought to be making a little counter medicine, I expect."

"But what can he do?"

"Find out if it's true or not."

She looked up anxiously. "Can he do that? If he does, Tom. . . ."

Tom smiled. "He can try, but I don't think he'll get much done. Y'see, Paw's got Herb and Eb and a couple more fellers down at the lawyer's place waiting for him to show up. Paw's going to retain him, as he calls it, to work for us."

"Well, but Jeff Smalley's no dunce, Tom."

"No one said he was. Right now it's first come first served, and we're going to make it a point to be first come *and* first served." Tom shifted his feet. "Joyce, I think I'd best get down that way just in case I'm wanted."

"All right," she said. "But where's your father now?"

"Paw and our friends are down at the stage office. Herb, Eb, and the rest are waiting at the lawyer's, like I told you."

He left her standing in the walkway and strode southward. People who recognized him nodded, those who didn't stepped aside. Joyce was motionless, watching him go. Her hands were clasped tightly before a flat stomach. There was a current of tightness in her that made even eating difficult.

When Tom passed the Running Horse, he ignored the three men lounging back against its wall, but instinct warned him they were Smalley's hands. Three heads turned as he swung by. Three appraising sets of eyes measured him.

Herb and the middle brother Eb nodded when Tom stopped near them. Herb was frowning darkly. "I've been telling Eb," he said, "we ought to go hunt the lawyer up. I buttonholed that farrier and he said the lawyer's got a stump ranch south of town, just off the road."

"We've been through that," Tom said. "Some of the fellows rode out there last night and his woman told them he'd gone to see some client. She didn't know where, or when he'd be back."

"But maybe he'll go home first," Herb said.

Tom nodded at him. "He might. I sent Slim down to watch for him right after he caught Jameson this morning. If he comes back to his house, Slim'll fetch him along."

Herb's scowl left. He looked down the walkway "Who're those monkeys outside Smalley's saloon?"

"Look like hammerheads to me," Tom said.

"A left-hand gun on any of 'em?" Eb asked.

Tom shook his head. "I looked for that. No."

While the three of them were standing there idly, looking northward, Jeff Smalley came out onto the plank walk. One of the loungers said something to him. Smalley turned leisurely and stared southward, saw the three Bosworths in front of the lawyer's place. After a moment he started toward them and without a word the three loungers fell in behind him.

By now Vacaville knew trouble was in the air. People grouped here and there, talking. Women caught up children and dragged them away. The saddle maker across the road was standing in his doorway, watching. Sean O'Brien came popping out of the narrow opening between the saddler's shop and Jameson's livery barn. He wore a filthy, shiny, mule-hide apron and his arms were bare and mighty. He squinted in a surly way, up and down the road.

J.B. Murphy, proprietor of the Vacaville Emporium, darted a quick look up and down the walk. He scuttled around a pickle barrel and hurriedly closed two heavy oak shutters across his solitary glass window.

Smalley and his friends kept on walking.

Across the road and down a ways a heavy-featured man with a fleshy body emerged from the sheriff's office, stopped stock-still on the walk, and stared. His soft body quivered an instant, then he whirled and disappeared inside the building again.

At the stage office, several doors down on the same side of the road, a slouched man at the door drew backward quickly, was lost to sight inside. A moment later a quiet line of armed men filed out of the office. Four of the six held carbines nakedly.

Across the road one of Smalley's companions said something sharply and Jeff swung his head, saw the lined-up men with guns, down the street from the sheriff's office. His steps slowed.

The sheriff came out of his place in a flash of movement. The coarse deputy was behind him, his too-wide eyes bright and foolish-looking. They both started to cross the road, eyes fixed on the Bosworths and the approaching Smalley. Neither saw the men along the wall behind them.

Smalley stopped a few feet from Tom, eyed the three images of old Franklin Bosworth stonily. None of his customary bantering arrogance showed now. " 'Morning, Tom," Smalley said.

Bosworth nodded without speaking. There was a steady glow of watchfulness in his look.

"You boys down to see the lawyer?"

Another nod.

Smalley's three companions spread out a little in feigned carelessness. The Bosworths remained motionless.

"Want to record your paw's bill of sale in the stage business?"

Then Tom spoke. "What we're here for doesn't matter," he said.

Smalley's brittle grin showed.

The emaciated sheriff and his trailing deputy came up. Both were watching Smalley. The sheriff said: " 'Morning, what's up?"

Smalley didn't answer. His gaze clung to Tom's face. There was triumph in it. "Tom," he said genially, "your paw's got no partnership in the stage line."

"No? Go tell him that."

"Even if he's got a paper from Hawk," Smalley went on, "it's no good. Hawk's an outlaw. He's gone . . . escaped from jail, which makes him doubly outlawed."

Herb's dark color mounted. He lost a battle with himself against interrupting. "Doubly outlawed," he spat out scornfully. "Who the hell d'you think you're bluffing, Smalley?"

Jeff Smalley's eyes shifted a fraction. He took in the bleak and belligerent appearance of the youngest brother, then swung back to Tom again. "Guess your brother don't believe signs, does he, Tom."

"What signs?"

"The ones the feller left who robbed your paw. The boot marks and all. Hawk's sign, Tom. Did you look at his horse before he ran away?"

"No," Tom said.

"Well, the sheriff and I did. It was over at Jameson's barn.

The sheriff went up to your place and looked at the sign the robber left. Identical, Tom."

Tom got a sardonic expression on his face. "That was real thoughtful," he said. "Maybe someone borrowed his horse."

"And his boots?" Smalley said, his contemptuous grin becoming firmer. "Pretty hard to get a man's boots off him, without him knowing it."

Tom went silent. He looked at the three men behind and off to one side of Jeff Smalley. They were watching him like hawks, still as stone, unblinking, blank-faced. "All right, Jeff," he said. "If you're going to make a play, you'd better make it."

"Naw," Smalley said, "I'm just waiting for the lawyer like you are. What would I want to make a play for?"

Tom looked scornfully at Smalley. "Want to play your game right up to the last card, don't you? Suits me, but before you drop the pot, you'd better take a good look across the road."

Smalley didn't turn but the sheriff did. His breath made a sharp sound in the silence. Six statues over there, watching, listening, lined out so that about five feet was between each man. Sweat started out upon the sheriff's face although it was very pleasant under the overhang.

"I saw them," Smalley said. "What they're doing is against the law, Tom. There's a town ordinance about armed gangs." Smalley shrugged. "It isn't enforced, though, so long as folks don't make trouble."

Herb swore suddenly. Eb reached down and grasped the younger man's arm, held it in a grip of iron.

The deputy moved closer, massive jaw jutting outward, pouting little lips sucked flat. The sheriff shot him a quick scowl. He stopped and watched Herb antagonistically.

From across the road a deep-booming old voice called out.

"Jeff, get away from there. Turn around and walk away!"

The sheriff twisted his upper body awkwardly. Jeff Smalley

turned his head. None of the three Bosworth boys took their eyes off Smalley's toughs or Smalley.

"Go on," Franklin Bosworth said, and there was none of the usual warmth to his strong voice. "Move along before someone gets hurt."

Then the sheriff took a hand. "Watch yourself, Bosworth," he said sharply. "You start anything and it'll be your funeral."

Smalley gazed across the road, apparently the only one in the clutch by the lawyer's office who was completely calm and unaffected.

"Bosworth," he said, "what's this all about, mind telling me?"

Franklin Bosworth snorted sarcastically. "The time for playing's past, Jeff," he said. "You know cussed well what it's all about."

"The stage line? Well, what about it?"

"I bought half interest yesterday, from John Hawk."

"So I heard," Smalley said. "Well, if you did, all you've got to do is record the paper, isn't it?"

"That's exactly what I'm waiting around for, Smalley. That's why the boys are here. Now move along and don't bother them."

"That kind of talk . . . ," the sheriff began, but Smalley silenced him with a gesture.

For a long moment Jeff Smalley said nothing. His eyes ranged over the men standing along the far wall with Franklin Bosworth. Some of them he knew, some were only familiar in a vague way, but there were five of them, six counting old Bosworth. And in front of him were the old man's big sons. Opposite them were the sheriff and his deputy. Behind him were his three hirelings. It didn't take Jeff Smalley but a moment to decide that whatever happened he was not only outnumbered and outmaneuvered, he was also the first man who would fall, if not from bullets opposite him, then very likely from the guns of those across from him.

Slow wrath burned steadily deep inside him. None of it showed in his face. He even affected a humorless grin. "All right, Bosworth," he said pleasantly. "I don't think you've got any such paper myself, but you can sure have it recorded for all I care. The stage's Curt's, not mine."

He turned without looking even at his men and walked back southward as far as the Running Horse, went through the louvered doors out of sight. Shortly afterward a bartender swept through the doors, apron clinging to his legs, walked in a hurrying and hunched-over way across the sparkling road and was lost from sight in the livery barn.

Franklin Bosworth spoke to the men around him. They went back inside the stage office. The old man stumped through the dust over to where his sons were. Tom was watching the livery barn. He gave his father the most perfunctory of nods and returned to his vigil.

When the bartender and Curt Jameson emerged from the shadows and started diagonally across the roadway, Tom grunted. "Look there," he said. "Jeff's fixing to figure a way out of this."

His father watched the hurrying figures a moment. "Not out," he said bluntly, "in. Jeff's no quitter whatever else he is. This hasn't blown over by a long shot."

Herb stepped away from the building, craned his neck to see if Smalley's hammerheads were still in sight. One was lounging before the saloon, apparently half asleep. "Let's get us a couple of those," he said savagely.

Eb Bosworth made a disgusted sound deep in his throat. "Cut that out," he said to Herb. "You're going to get a bellyful of fighting before this is over."

Their father watched the sheriff walk away with the deputy trailing him like a dog. "Boys," he said, "we've got to find Hawk. We can't stall off a showdown much longer. Jeff'll be hatching real trouble now. If he finds out I'm running a whizzer on him, we won't have a leg to stand on."

Tom looked around. "Well," he said, "what can he do about it if he does find out?"

Franklin Bosworth looked at his son. "Do?" he said. "Why, he can have that gutless sheriff arrest the lot of us, for one thing. The other thing is he can hold us long enough to give his left-handed gunman a couple days' head start to get here."

"We can get the seven thousand back," Herb said shortly. "I'll personally take it from Smalley if I get half a chance."

"The seven thousand," their father said, "isn't half as important to me as getting Hawk cleared. As far as the seven thousand is concerned, I don't expect to get it back in cash."

"How then?" Herb asked.

"By getting Jameson's interest in the stage line," Franklin Bosworth said. "I figured on that after Hawk told us how the wind was blowing. You see, I'd invest that much in the line anyway, so one way or another I'd have half interest. If I got the cash back, I'd buy Jameson out. If I don't get it back I'll wring a bill of sale out of him and let him worry about the money."

Tom was listening to his father but watching the sheriff cross the road toward his office. "I don't think wringing a bill of sale out of Jameson'd be hard right now."

"No," his father said, "but right now what we've got to do is find John Hawk. Without him we're sort of like a stage without horses. He's the one to lead this war, boys."

"The Lord knows where he is," Herb said, caustically disgruntled.

But Franklin Bosworth, the self-styled judge of men, was confident. "He'll be along," he said. "Meanwhile, I'm going to the Porters'. You bring that lawyer fellow down there as soon's he's corralled. And Tom . . . keep an eye on things. So long as we're on both sides of the road as strong as we are, I don't think they'll try too much."

When he started away, Eb moved up beside him. "I'd best go along," he said, but his father motioned him back with a wry look.

"Odd, I've been able to get around by myself for over sixty years," he said, "and now, all of a sudden, I'm unable to. Never mind about me. Eb, just stay with your brothers. I'll be in plain sight until I get to the Porters'. No one'll try anything as long as they know you fellows are watching. See you in a little," he said, and walked down the plank walk.

The town was hushed in a grip of expectancy. When Franklin Bosworth went by the Emporium, he saw J.B. Murphy peering at him. He nodded gravely to him.

In front of the Running Horse the remaining tough was watching the roadway in a hooded-eyed, leisurely way. At the elder Bosworth's approach he looked up, past the big figure to the distant faces southward, also watching. When the rancher went by, he nodded. The gunman nodded back just as serenely.

From within the Running Horse came voices, indistinct but packed with excitement. Bosworth heard and strained to make out words. He couldn't because Jameson and Smalley were in the gambling room off the bar. The distance was too great in spite of Smalley's grinding tones.

And Jeff Smalley was furious. "Why the hell didn't you tell me all that yesterday," he was saying. "Do you think I'd have let him ride out of here if I'd known all that? Jameson, you damned fool, that feller knows too much to live."

"You said you sent Chet after him," Jameson said shrilly.

"Sure, just like I did after the other one, you idiot, but only to make sure he went south, not to gun him."

"But if he comes back, Chet'll gun him, won't he?"

"I didn't *tell* him too," Smalley said fiercely. "Chet's as bad as you are that way. If he isn't *told* to do something, he doesn't do it." Smalley turned, perched upon a table, and stared hard at the far wall. "Lord, why'd I ever trust you, anyway!"

"I'd have told you, Jeff. . . ."

"You'd have told me! Why didn't you then? Curt, if Hawk knows all the things he said to you, there's one hell of a good chance he *did* give old Bosworth a bill of sale. Do you realize that?"

Jameson was making a shaky cigarette. He didn't raise his head or answer.

"And if he did . . . you bonehead . . . if he did, Bosworth'll do just what he told you in the barn. He'll refuse to approve the mail contract, not to mention the Army transportation contract. Know what that'll do, don't you? Put us plumb out of the bidding, that's what it'll do."

"Well, we can get other. . . ."

"In time for the bidding?" Smalley demanded. "Curt, you're crazy!"

Smalley got away from the table. "I ought to let Bosworth have you," he said savagely. "Ought to let them string you up. Bad enough you're gutless but a damned sight worse when you let Hawk slip away knowing what he knows. It wouldn't surprise me a bit if the U.S. marshal rode in here now."

Smalley's rage subdued Curt Jameson. He lit the bulky cigarette twice before he got it going, then he forgot to draw on it, and it went out again, hung forgotten in his mouth.

CHAPTER EIGHT

The countryside glowed with fresh vitality as John Hawk rode through it. Summer's spell of long lassitude was broken and briefly, before winter came gray and leaden, fall glistened with the brittleness of glass. The dryness of the air, cleansed of dust, of heat waves, brought the world into sharp focus. Sounds carried. Distance was spanned. The air was fragrant with a distinct sharpness, a bracing clarity.

He rode easy and light in the saddle, hope riding with him as strong as the day was sparkling.

Coming into the southern roadway, trailing past like frayed rope, miles below Vacaville, he stopped to look and listen. Nothing stirred. There was no sound. He rode northward along the road and let his horse pick its way. There would be no reason to hide yet. He rode with his head swinging, eyes alive, and saw underfoot two sets of tracks going southward. Fresh tracks, one set fresher than the other.

He stopped. He sat bent a little, studying the ground, and a cold thrill ran through him. The first tracks he recognized as his own, Sean O'Brien's new shoes. And those other tracks had been made shortly after he'd passed, last night, by another horse going southward.

Where he'd left the roadway the night before, he now made a quartering movement. And found that the other tracks had left the road at the same spot. He had been followed.

Instinct chilled him. He straightened in the saddle and reined off the road. He rode steadily until he was deep in a maze of game trails among prickly chaparral. There he stopped, got down, and walked stealthily back, for whoever had trailed him the night before could conceivably still be trailing him.

But why? What purpose could a man have, tracking him? Did Jeff Smalley imagine John might lead one of his men to a cache? He stood beside the back trail, watching, listening, thinking. Possibly, maybe that was it. Smalley thought he might have something hidden. Or Smalley may have just wanted to assure himself that John Hawk *had* headed for Mexico. If so, why? What did Smalley or Jameson care after they'd got rid of him? They were safe enough. And if they'd doubted, why hadn't they used the assassin's way when he was escaping? It would have looked very logical, a dead escapee named John Hawk killed while breaking out of jail. Most natural thing in the world.

So he'd been followed either to make sure he left the country or because someone thought he might have a cache somewhere. Something they could follow him to and, if it was worthwhile, kill him over. Whichever it was, whatever the purpose of the phantom trailer, the important question was—where was he now?

He waited almost an hour but there was nothing. Nearly convinced the man had stayed behind in Springerville, he returned to his horse, mounted, and strained for sight or sound. Nothing, just the clearness of dry air. No sounds of any kind.

An eeriness grew in him, the inherited awareness from dim ancestors that responded to being watched, to the knowledge that he *was* being watched. Then the man was still out there somewhere.

John rode farther into the scrub. His horse was reluctant for the chaparral was dense and barbed. Deer fled ahead of him, rabbits scurried. He pushed through the undergrowth in a westerly fashion, then, later, swung due north. After that he had to guess his position in relation to Vacaville and shortly after noon he thought the town was a little behind and east of him.

Riding, he considered ways of making the shadow show itself. When he burst out of the brush, he rode across a waving expanse of curing grass, and knew his shadow must follow eventually.

Lack of familiarity with the land hampered him, so he headed for Hunter's Spring. That area at least he was passably familiar with.

Once he topped a little knoll and waited there, watching. Whoever the man was, he was as elusive as an Apache, for even in the open places nothing showed.

At Hunter's Spring he dismounted, made a cigarette, and smoked it. Ground it out and walked northward a ways, in the direction he'd first seen Jack Keeney riding, that day when he'd stolen the Bosworth horses.

There was a rough rise to the ground northward. In the distance he recognized the ridge he and Joyce had sat upon that time when they'd first ridden together. Trees began to stand out, starkly clear, rich and bountiful-looking. He walked toward them, catching their fragrance. Walked northward until a strong lip of land, corroded and steep, lay in his path. Then he stopped, faced back, and stared hard down the long incline. The view was like something cut from ice, so clear and unmarred with atmospheric distortions, haziness.

And waited. With fear beginning to reach him. The man was more ghost than flesh. He never crossed a clearing, never rode bobbingly above the brush patches. Never showed himself, and therefore he must be all imagination.

John turned a little, looking westward, for there was a chance that the stranger had paralleled him. Ridden farther northward than John had in order to be above him. He swept the distance and the closeness for signs of movement and quite suddenly out of the corner of his eye caught the glisten of metal. A vibrating burst of warning exploded in his mind. He was falling, letting himself fall almost before it was clear.

He lay flat, head twisted far around, eyes locked upon that high, corroded eminence. There was no glistening.

He rolled into the unkempt shadow of a juniper tree and stayed there. He'd seen gun metal, and then he hadn't. So that's where the stranger was, up above him. He had withdrawn his gun at the last moment for some inexplicable reason and had failed to fire.

John squinted. The distance was great but not too great. A carbine could reach him from that far. Thinking like that he became acutely conscious of his own disarmed state. Any man in his position who would attempt to outsmart or outfight an armed man was insane. He slowly got his legs under him and worked his way backward, deeper into the shadows until he had a great depth of them between him and the man atop the drop-off. There was just one solution—flee.

Then he scuttled through the sparkling clearness from brush to tree to rock until he was winded, down by Hunter's Spring where that deep-scarred name, cut with agonizing despair into the living limestone, mocked him.

He got astride and rode swiftly. Springerville was too far and Vacaville too close. He rode in the only other direction he knew of, toward the upland country Joyce had shown him, toward the vaguely recalled empire of Bosworth's Pothook.

The afternoon was turning rose-colored when he drew up for the last time. He looked, knowing it was senseless to do so. After that one pause he rode all the way to the Pothook before drawing rein again, and there, a man challenged him.

"Hold up there! What y'want here?"

"Franklin Bosworth," John said, "and quick."

The man stalked closer. He was afoot and by looks was an ir-

142

rigator, a chore boy, or a handy man of some kind. He was old and grizzled with secretive eyes hidden within folding pouches of flesh.

"Ain't a male Bosworth on the place," he said. "They's all went to Vacaville yestiddy and none of 'em been home since. Lady's at the house. I'll take ye."

John followed.

The "lady" turned out to be three women, the wives of Franklin, Tom, and Eb. John touched his hat and in a single breath said his name, and that he'd like to borrow both a pistol and a carbine. The younger women stood motionlessly but the older woman moved gracefully and swiftly as though everyone who came to the ranch needed armament. She emerged from the house with a cradled carbine and a naked six-gun, handed them to John without a word, and took a long look at his face.

"I know who you are," she said, "but this is the first time we've ever met."

John smiled broadly at her, partly in relief, partly at the oddness of their meeting. "You're Franklin's wife," he said.

"Yes, and you're Joyce Porter's friend."

He had holstered the handgun and now he sat up there, gazing down at her with the carbine in his fist. "I've sure been working at it," he said, and the younger women both smiled. The snapping eyes of Franklin's wife were unmoved.

"The men're still in town. From what I can imagine, Mister Hawk, I'd reckon you'd best go down to them there."

"I will," John said, "but there's a man trailing me."

"Oh, that's why you needed the guns."

"Yes'm."

"All right," the older woman said bleakly. "You go on to town, and if he comes around here, he'll get what for."

John wheeled his horse and loped out of the yard, straight down his back trail. There was a power of strength flowing into him from the weight and sag of guns.

He rode all the way to Vacaville and didn't see a single soul.

The town was dead in the soft light of afternoon. People, the few he saw, were far from the main business section, and when he loped boldly through the clear air, someone called his name in a sharp, incisive way.

"John!"

He pulled up and looked across where she stood.

"Come over here!"

He went, sat forward a little, looking into her face. He saw strickened whiteness, the immensity of eyes with fear darkening their depths.

"Get down. Don't sit up there for all the world to shoot at!"

He dismounted, still holding the carbine, and she went through the gate to take his arm, pull him back into the yard with her. "Go inside," she said. "Uncle Frank and Herb are in there with my father and the lawyer."

"Oh, all right. But where are the others? They weren't at the ranch."

She heard the slow-walking gait of a horseman southward and the fingers on his arm tightened. "Hurry. Tom and Eb are at the stage office with the others, waiting. Hurry, please . . . !" She put force into her hold as though to drag him. He moved, went with her as far as the porch steps, and turned when a rider went past out on the road. He turned and gazed into the wide, troubled eyes of the Texas gunman. He knew who his private phantom had been.

"*Please*, John!"

"Sure," he said without moving, watching the rider until a building cut him off and only the sounds of his careless walking horse were heard. "All right."

The lawyer was standing, his back to the dead fireplace, his sad, dark eyes tired and anxious, his slight body ridiculous among those titans. When John entered with Joyce behind him, Franklin Bosworth stood up quickly, astonished and relieved at the same time. Judge Porter nodded without greeting and pushed up another chair. Herb Bosworth nodded at John; he looked sullenly dissatisfied and under some invisible restraint.

The lawyer cleared his throat and gazed sardonically at John. "If you'd be good enough to give Mister Bosworth a bill of sale to your interest in the Vacaville-Springerville Stage Company," he said, "I believe a lot of the present tension could be negated."

John blinked at him.

Franklin Bosworth explained what the lawyer was talking about how he'd held their enemies at bay with a ruse by claiming he had bought John's interest in the line.

Somewhere in the rear of the house someone was making noises with cups and saucers.

"Yes," John said, "of course. Who's got a piece of paper?"

Judge Porter leaned over from his desk and offered a tablet. The lawyer had a pen ready. "Write as I dictate," he said, and looked sidewise at the judge who was studying Joyce's "friend" with a solemn and expressionless regard.

The lawyer talked. Words ran smoothly, blurred into a song of professional verbiage while John wrote swiftly with his bared head low, and when Joyce came in with a large tray piled with cups, saucers, and a graniteware coffee pot, the only man who ignored her was John.

"That's all," the lawyer said, and smiled at Joyce.

John re-read the paper and handed it to the judge, who also read it before the lawyer got it, folded it carefully after having Joyce witness and sign it, and put it into his pocket.

"Coffee," the lawyer said. "I need this." And he poured himself a steaming black cup of it. Over the cup's edge he said to Franklin Bosworth: "I suppose you know this won't do anything more than bring on the fight?"

Before Bosworth could answer, John said: "Tell me all that's happened since yesterday, please."

So they told him, only Joyce and her father remaining silent. Even Herb spoke, angrily and with a cold ring to his voice. He finished with: "So Tom and the others are over at the office . . . on that side of the road . . . and we're up here on this side of the road. And Smalley's with Jameson somewhere, probably in the saloon. Everything's simmering, Hawk. The first one to sneeze'll start a war."

Judge Porter leaned back. His chair squeaked. "It's not that bad, surely," he said. "If I thought it was, I'd send for the marshal."

Herb showed his teeth. "For all the good it'd do," he said, "you might as well send for Old Scratch."

Franklin looked over at his son with the ice-blue gaze totally without humor in it. Herb subsided like Tom had done under that silent rebuke.

John looked at Joyce.

She seemed stiff, unnatural as she returned his look with one of dry fear, dread. But she said nothing and the faint haze of tobacco smoke softened her face enough to make it appear more distant from John than ever. He turned to the others. Franklin Bosworth was addressing her father. The judge's leonine head was thrown back a little as though he needed the extra elevation to see better.

"Self-defense. Regardless, Judge, I want you to know . . . and everyone else present here . . . that when we leave this house we do so peacefully inclined."

"I'm sure of that," Judge Porter said. "And while I've heard rumors about the sheriff, I've also heard rumors about everyone in this room at one time or another and I put no faith in any rumor."

"Believe as you will," Franklin Bosworth said. "The fact

146

remains that we have violated no law by being in town today, nor do we intend to violate any. So, if the law attempts to arrest any of us, it can only be doing so because Jeff Smalley has ordered it to. Under those circumstances, Judge, my men will resist. I will resist."

The judge leaned upon his desk and his face was drawn. "Listen, Franklin," he said. "We're too old for this sort of thing, you and me. Besides that we're too close. So let me say this. If the law tries to arrest you, don't resist. Let them take you." He bobbed his head at the lawyer. "He'll have you out on a writ in twenty minutes. I'll vouch and sign for you, both. But, Franklin, if you resist, it's a felony, and for resisting alone you can be imprisoned. Now for heaven's sake don't make this situation any worse." The direct eyes went to John and stayed there. The judge seemed to be balancing some thought. "Mister Hawk, what I've been trying to do here this afternoon is preserve the peace. I'll ask you as I've asked the others with Mister Bosworth . . . do not be the first to draw a gun."

"I won't be," John said dryly, "mainly because I never was very fast with one."

The lawyer chuckled. Even Herb, caught in the grimness of his thoughts, was jarred into a smile. Only Joyce looked at him without humor.

"Then you ought to stay right here," she said, and at that even the judge smiled.

Judge Porter stood up. "All right, Franklin, your attorney will file the bill of sale and I can assure you it's legal whether Jeff Smalley thinks it is or not." In a brief show of exasperation the judge added: "How the devil does he think men in prison sell land and buy things, anyway?"

The lawyer crossed the room as far as the door, then he stopped. "This way?" he asked dubiously, and Herb Bosworth made a growling noise as he pushed up closer and put one big fist around the knob.

"This way, and I hope they're out there, waiting."

"John?"

He stood up, looking across the room at her. "Yes?"

The judge and Franklin Bosworth looked at them both, then moved toward the door. She moved behind them swiftly, heading toward the kitchen. John followed. He was going through the opening when she turned, almost causing him to collide with her.

"Don't go! Please don't go, John."

"Now, Joyce. . . ."

"There'll be a fight, John."

Looking solemnly at her he was inclined to agree but he said: "They'd be fools to start one. Counting me, Bosworth's got eleven men loaded for bear."

"How *can* you be so naïve?" she demanded. "If he had a hundred . . . it only takes one bullet."

"This is my fight, remember?"

She half turned from him. "I wish I'd never seen you . . . sometimes men are so brutal."

"When you must," he said, "you fight fire with fire. I started this. I've got to be in at the finish."

She whirled back. "Whose finish . . . your own?"

He was uncomfortable. "Somebody's," he said vaguely. "Now, Joyce, you're getting all upset."

"When I'm with you," she mocked him, "things never seem to turn out like I'd imagined they would. Do you remember saying that?"

"Yes, but now wait a. . . ."

"And they never will, either."

"I wouldn't say that. You're as white as a ghost, Joyce. Let's not argue now."

"Arguing? Whose arguing? I'm pleading, John."

"Look at it my way. This is the showdown on something I started. Something I forced to come out like this, and for just one reason, Joyce . . . you."

"I wish you hadn't!"

He stood in awkward silence for a moment. "If I hadn't, I'd have been just another cowboy, another drifter, and you'd have never seen me for dust."

"Yes, I would have," she said fiercely. "I saw you that day I took my horse across to Mister O'Brien. And do you want to know the rest of it? I saw you standing on the walk up by the café. I put a stone in my horse's frog and led him across the road so you'd see *me*. When you did, you crossed the road and just happened to be standing by the corral when I went past. I got a good look at you then, John, and I thought you were handsome, so I stopped a minute to talk to a man I knew, thought you'd screw up your nerve to talk to me then, but you didn't." She stood there, looking directly at him with high color and a quiver down around her mouth. "Is there anything else you'd like to know?"

He blinked at her and very slowly burned a dark crimson. "Then . . . you knew I was faking when I came over to look at the horse?"

"I've already told you I knew that. And the ride up in the hills under the pines. . . ."

"Oh," he said in a small way.

"John, please. . . ."

He touched her, withdrew the hand, and let it hang disconsolately beside him. "It's got to be this way, Joyce. For both of us."

"But what'll happen?"

And before he understood quite how, he was kissing her. There was a hot dampness on his face where tears lay, from her, and a soft deliciousness to her mouth. A scent of squeaky

149

clean hair, and a booming call from the parlor. "John! Come on!"

He drew back, turned with the miniature of her white face etched forever under his heart, and walked back through the house. Judge Porter looked at him strangely. Franklin Bosworth's eyes widened a trifle and Herb twisted the knob. The door swung inward.

John went first, holding the carbine. Behind him was Herb Bosworth, and close to him his father, coattail tucked back to reveal a smoothly worn ivory gun butt. The last man to leave the house was the little lawyer, and farther back, framed in the doorway, face bleached and anxious, stood Judge Porter. Joyce was nowhere in sight.

They turned south on the plank walk with shivering echoes falling behind from their boot steps. They walked toward the lawyer's office in a tight group. No one opposed their passage. No one was in sight on the plank walks on either side of the road.

Vacaville lay hushed and inward, its back upon the towering beauty of the land. Bent over, it seemed, the better to watch the steady progress of the men behind John Hawk.

A raffish old mongrel with a stump wagging padded up to them and stopped. There was something in the air, something vital and sere that reached in and touched him icily. He stopped, snout up, poised and working, then he stood rigid for a moment and began a wide walk around the four men.

They were almost to the Running Horse *en route* to the lawyer's office when a man stood up from a nailed bench near the saloon's door. He watched a moment, bristling, then turned and faded from sight through the louvered doors.

Across the way an indolent figure making a cigarette straightened up, cigarette forgotten, sharp eyes watching. The man let the paper trough slide through his fingers. Its flakes of dry tobacco cascaded downward. A turn of the head, a short, explosive sentence backward, and other men began filing out of the stage office. Tom Bosworth led them. Behind him was the bony-faced Bosworth rider and behind him came more men until the last one stood briefly framed in the opening. Cleve, drained of color, lips wet and sick-looking, was holding a company sawed-off shotgun with both hands.

Abreast of the Running Horse, John turned his head enough to watch the doors. Over them a white face appeared. Two pair of eyes met and held and recognized one another. John and the Texas killer. It occurred to John that the louvered doors were all that kept hell from breaking loose, for behind him Herb Bosworth stalked with a red froth of antagonism motivating him. All that was needed was for Herb to glimpse that left-hand gun.

No one interrupted their march to the lawyer's office, but when they finally got there, the lawyer couldn't unlock his door. Of such ludicrous things are heroics made. John took the key and twisted it in the lock. The door opened inward.

The room was stuffy and musty-smelling. The others pushed in behind John until the office was full of big bodies. Then the lawyer ran a limp handkerchief around his face and sank into a chair.

"Good Lord," he said almost in a whisper. "That was terrible. Unbelievable. I had no idea the walk was so long."

"What do you have to do, now?" John asked, unmoved.

"Record it. Attach a notification of legal compliance to it and send it to Raton to be recorded."

"Send it to Raton? I thought you could record it right here."

"No, all I can do here is make an exact copy and retain it for local files. The original must be sent to Raton for entry there into the territory's. . . ."

"Suppose it never reaches Raton?"

"That would be too bad, Mister Hawk, but no great damage

would be done. You see, so long as the copy exists and the principals are available in the event we must make another document, the original isn't essential. But I've never had one of those things get. . . ."

"You never tried to send anything with so many enemies over my stage line, either," John said, and turned to face Franklin Bosworth. "We could send a man south with it," he suggested.

But Bosworth vetoed it with a head shake. "I've a hunch," he said, "by the time the next mail goes out . . . with that paper . . . there'll either be no sense in sending it at all or there won't be anyone left in Vacaville sufficiently interested in who owns the stage company to risk stopping a coach to get that thing."

Herb crossed the room to the door, stood there peering out. Without facing back, he said: "Tom's over there . . . Tom and the rest of them, Paw."

"In that case," Bosworth said, gazing downward at the lawyer, "I don't reckon you'd care to join us in a little fresh air?"

The lawyer didn't even shake his head, he just stared at the old man with his cheeks quivering.

John switched the carbine to his right arm again. "Where to now?" he asked.

"Let's go see Curt Jameson," Bosworth said, and they left the office.

Incongruously someone, somewhere, started a nickelodeon playing. Its music smashed into the stillness with all the force of a screaming crowd.

They cut diagonally across the deserted roadway toward Jameson's livery barn. Only one thing had changed. Jeff Smalley was standing on the walk in front of the Running Horse. He had a cigar between his teeth and fanned out on both sides of him were seven men, all as motionless as Smalley was. Eight faces turning as the Bosworth faction went by, following them to the maw of the livery barn, and after they disappeared inside

Jeff Smalley spoke to the hooded-eyed man directly behind him, partially hidden from sight.

"Up on the roof, Chet, and wait."

"You got a signal?" the Texan asked.

"Yeah, the first shot."

"Any one of them in particular?"

"Two. Hawk and Bosworth, in that order."

And the gunman disappeared through the louvered doors.

Across the way Jameson's hostler was holding his bristly broom like it was salvation, tightly and close to his body.

John said: "Where's Jameson?"

"He went out the back way."

"When?"

"Just now, in a hurry."

They moved on, spread out in skirmish order, through the gloomy interior of the barn, and John spoke aside to Franklin Bosworth.

"I've a notion he's hiding at the farrier's shop. I'll go back outside and down the slit between the buildings, get behind O'Brien's place, and if he comes out when you fellows go in the front way, I'll nail him."

Bosworth nodded without speaking and moved to close the gap left in their line as John turned back.

Outside was a deep silence; the nickelodeon had stopped. He shot a glance toward the Running Horse. The only blur of surreptitious movement came from beside the high and square false front above the saloon. Without looking closer, John ducked around the edge of the barn and hurried down the narrow passageway. He emerged among the scrap iron by the horseshoeing shop, and waited. There was no movement. He sidled along the rear of an adjoining building until he was behind O'Brien's, then he faded into shadows, and again waited.

Men were coming. A soft sound of spurs, of boots treading

153

upon metal things, a heightening of the quiver in the air. Then voices.

"Where's Jameson?"

"Get out of here!"

The sound of a solid blow, a crumpling body, and John knew who had fallen, who had struck O'Brien down. He could picture the fierceness of Herb Bosworth's face, then something moved along the back of the shop and he kneeled, raised the carbine, and tracked it down the sights. When the still dinginess parted enough for him to make out a shape, he cocked the gun. Its working mechanism sounded extra loud. The bulky shape stopped, frozen.

"Put your hands over your head, Jameson. Now move out into the light."

He stood up and uncocked the gun, walked forward, and saw the naked soul of a man and was repelled by it. "Turn around. Walk toward the front of the shop."

Herb Bosworth reached out as Jameson went by and snaked the pistol out of his waistband, threw it on a coal pile beside a rusted forge.

Franklin Bosworth's right hand was curled around the ivory butt of his belt gun. "No time to waste, Jameson," he said. There was no trace of the warmth in his voice now, only the immovable calmness. "I want another bill of sale to the stage line."

Herb reached out in contempt and slapped Jameson's arms down from above his head.

"I want it right now."

Jameson's face was gray, his lips blue and moving. "I won't," he said. That and no more.

John raised his eyes from the bent body of Sean O'Brien in time to see the older man give Herb a significant signal. The younger Bosworth went rummaging through the shop, returned with a stout hard-twist rope. Ignoring Jameson, he sought about overhead for a suitable tie beam, found one, and cast the loose end of the rope over it, caught it with his free hand, and set to work fashioning a noose.

Knowing Herb's state of mind, his willingness, John looked at Franklin. There was nothing to see in that seamed, expressionless face except the ice-blue eyes. He moved up closer, stepping over Sean O'Brien to do so.

"They aren't bluffing," he said to Jameson.

"They wouldn't dare," Jameson answered, trembling. Herb looked up with wildness in his gaze, and laughed.

"Listen, Jameson," John said with belief growing in him that they would, "do what he said and save your neck."

"It's stealing."

"You won't be around to say so," Franklin said pointedly.

"Come on, Jameson," John urged, conviction becoming certainty. "Besides, you're not losing, you're gaining."

"No."

"You got back the seven thousand plus my five."

"That's a lie!"

"You got half of the seven and all of my five . . . unless you've already split with Smalley. Anyway, the line's not worth half, let alone your life."

"The law'll protect. . . ."

"You won't be here to sign a complaint," Herb interrupted, moving forward with the rope held out.

Jameson threw up both arms to fend him off. Herb transferred the rope to one hand and lashed outward. The sound was like a small pistol exploding. Jameson's knees buckled. He would have fallen except for John's grasp. A rattling sound came out of his throat.

John shook him until the cloudiness left his eyes, then forced him to stand.

Herb put the rope around his neck, snugged its roughness up

against the fat man's flesh. Franklin Bosworth was like a graven statue, both arms crossed over his chest.

John shook the livery man until his dazed look left. He bent toward him.

"This is your last chance, Jameson."

"I'll write it," Jameson said. "Take the rope off."

And John did.

Herb looked disappointed. He remained close to the fat man with anger mottling his skin.

Then Franklin Bosworth moved, came forward with a pencil in one hand and a pad of soiled paper in the other. Jameson took them and leaned forward toward a resurfaced anvil's smooth plane. His hand shook uncontrollably. He bit his lower lip and twisted his body to hide the shaking. Franklin Bosworth quoted the other bill of sale from memory, and Jameson wrote.

Herb tossed the rope aside.

Sean O'Brien groaned. John looked down. There was a spreading welt along his jaw. Where his head had landed in the dirt, a small stone was crimson and shiny with blood. He stooped over and shook the farrier, watched his sullen eyes focus, then aided him to his feet. O'Brien fell against a tie post and leaned there, breathing loudly for a long time.

"Read it back," Franklin Bosworth said, and Jameson's wavering words droned.

O'Brien seemed to rally from the sound. He lifted his head and stared around him, let the watery gaze settle upon Jameson for a while before it moved to Franklin, then to John, and finally to Herb. The younger Bosworth returned it with hostility, and when O'Brien licked his lips, Herb said: "Next time keep a civil tongue in your head."

O'Brien's face darkened weakly, his knuckles grew white, but he said nothing.

Jameson held the paper out and Franklin took it, put it carefully in a coat pocket, and said: "You'll have to come along with us, I reckon, for this'll have to be witnessed and so forth by the lawyer."

"Across the road?" Jameson said. "No, I can't do it."

Herb took his arm in a mighty grip and half propelled, half carried him, back toward the livery barn and the roadway beyond where the dying light of day painted the dust red with bold strokes.

CHAPTER NINE

Late afternoon brought an earlier than usual shading of dusk to Vacaville. A tingling chill set in and moved outward as the sun slowly sank. The near side of the road, westerly, was shadowed but enough light still lived to limn the far side. From within the barn Herb's strong footfalls sounded solidly as he pushed Jameson along. The liveryman's breath was scratchy, irregular.

John moved to the right as far as box stalls would permit. He scanned the opposite roadway, seeking men, and just before he came close to the opening he saw them, fanned out as the Bosworth faction had been earlier, spread wide with distance between them on either side of the Running Horse Saloon's doors. He checked his stride and called to Herb.

"Hold it. They're out there like a firing squad."

But Herb kept on going, pushing Curt Jameson. Over his shoulder he said: "That's what I came here for." And his father moved faster, coming up on Herb's right side.

John caught up then. He cocked the carbine softly. Over the sound he heard footfalls, two sets of them, coming down the plank walk on their side of the road. That time Franklin spoke.

"Stop!"

Herb stopped within plain sight of the men lining the opposite side of the road. John could feel sweat start out on his body. The footsteps kept coming, and when the tall, thin figure hove into view, the face topping it was rigid and pale.

"Hawk! I want you!"

The sheriff stopped. His deputy stepped to one side of him, behind, his dull features twisted a little.

"Put that gun down!"

Herb, handling Curt Jameson like he was a wet sack, shoved him forward. "Here," he said, "you want lawbreakers so bad, here's one. Take him."

The sheriff's eyes never flickered from John. "Put that gun down, Hawk!"

Then Franklin Bosworth spoke. "Sheriff, I want to swear out a warrant against Jameson here. Charges to be armed robbery, assault. That'll do for a starter."

"I'm warning you, Hawk," the sheriff said, unheeding.

John shook his head. "I'll look you up in an hour or so," he said. "Right now I'm busy."

"That's resisting, Hawk."

John felt his face grimace a smile. "It won't matter," he said. "If you're right, I'll have the whole book tossed at me anyway. One more charge won't make a hell of a lot of difference."

"I'll disarm you," the sheriff said, but he made no move.

"That would be a mistake," John said.

And Herb added: "Maybe even your last mistake, Smalley man. You want to arrest somebody so bad, here, take this carrion. I'm tired of holding him up." He gave Jameson a slight shove but didn't release his hold on the liveryman's arm.

The sheriff's thin face got red. "I'm empowered," he said, "to use force to take you, Hawk."

And for the first time that afternoon Franklin Bosworth laughed. It wasn't an agreeable sound. "I've been wondering," he said, "just how Jeff was going to justify starting a war. Well, go ahead, Sheriff, walk over there and deputize his hammerheads. At least it'll make things a little more even. He's got seven men lined up. You and the fathead behind will make nine. Smalley'll make ten. That's fair enough. We've also got ten men."

The sheriff finally shot the old man a look. "There's a warrant for you, too, Bosworth."

Herb swore explosively. "Why don't you try and arrest him?"

The sheriff stood in silence for a moment longer, then he said loudly: "All right. The two of you are resisting arrest, and I'm authorized to deputize a posse." He turned abruptly and started across the road. Dust squirted under his footfalls.

Someone deep in the barn said: "Steady, fellows. It's me, Tom."

John wanted to turn but he didn't. Tom strode up where they stood facing Smalley's crew, watching the sheriff's back as he stiffly and loudly swore in the seven gunmen as deputies.

"Paw, you want us all down here?"

Franklin spoke with his gun in his fist, thumb lying crooked over the hammer. "No, Tom. You fellows stay down by the office."

"We'll be split up," Tom said. "It'd be better, I think, if we were all together. They might rush you fellows in here."

"That would be a mistake," John said, "trying to cross the road after us."

"Well . . . ?" Tom asked.

"Go on back, Tom," his father said, "and when they fire the first shot, don't wait. Cut into them with all you have."

"All right, but I'll leave you one man, anyway."

Tom went back down the dingy corridor of the livery barn.

John heard someone moving flat-footedly and without spurs behind him. He darted a look, saw Cleve with the double-barreled, sawed-off shotgun. He caught only the briefest glimpse of an ill-appearing face, then looked forward again.

The sheriff was finishing. He had progressed along the line of men until he was close to the louvered doors of the Running Horse. John noticed that, even while he was searching for the Texan, Chet Cantrell, the gunman was not among the others.

At the saloon's doorway the lawman paused, and, as he did so, Jeff Smalley emerged, stood beside him listening to the sheriff's talk for a moment, then turned to gaze steadily at the five men in the large opening of the livery barn. Without raising his voice Smalley said: "Turn Jameson loose."

Franklin answered. "Come get him, Jeff."

Smalley was silent.

The sheriff was as stiff as a ramrod, his coarse-faced deputy like a shadow beside and slightly behind him. "Hawk and Bosworth . . . this is your last chance to put down those guns and surrender. That's a warning."

John called out: "The way things stand now, Sheriff, we'd be walking into hang ropes and you know it! Smalley told me that last night. For my part I'd rather go out this way, maybe take you with me."

Smalley said: "Hawk, you're a fool. You don't have a Chinaman's chance. I thought you were pretty smart until I heard you'd come back."

"You talk too damned much," Herb growled, shifting his hold on Jameson, "and so does your pardner here."

John could see Smalley's regard shift from young Bosworth to Jameson. It was hard to tell from that distance, but he thought Smalley's lips compressed a trifle. "I don't care what you do with him," Smalley said spitefully, and turned upon his heel, went back into the saloon.

John heard a sighing breath go out of Cleve behind him. "Get back," he said. "That shotgun won't carry that far. Don't even try to hit them unless they start across the road. Hear me, Cleve?"

"I hear you."

John's attention was caught by movement. Remembering the glimpse he'd had of something up by the false front, he squinted, concentrating, knowing a sniper was there.

The sheriff stepped down into the dust of the roadway.

A man yelled something incoherent, and the sheriff hesitated, risked a look southward where the noise had come from. Dust-laden riders were jogging stiffly into Vacaville from the farthest extremity of the town's limits. They were stiffly grim. Closer, up by the stage office, a rider called out a curse at the sheriff. His deputy turned, planted thick legs, and raised his pistol. It is very likely his mind being what it was, the gesture was simply meant to be threatening, but the situation was critical. They were men, not boys. To them a threatening gun meant fight. A single shot sounded, reverberations cascading down the roadway. The deputy staggered, dropped his gun, and sat down heavily in the manured roadway. Wounded, he appeared ridiculous instead of pathetic.

John saw movement again, a flash of it before the echoes had died. He saw the carbine barrel swing around the overhead false front and settle. He kneeled and fired. The hidden gunman let off his own shot from tangled reflexes, fingers that jerked when John's bullet splintered its way through the woodwork.

In a stark second John saw the gun barrel come over the louvered doors, saw the mushrooming blast come from it, and winced even as Curt Jameson threw up his arms without a sound, and sagged. Herb looked stunned, then let Jameson go and ducked back to the side of the barn.

"Killed him, by God," he said. "Jameson."

John understood instantly with a rare flash of perception. Jeff Smalley's opener had silenced his bungling partner.

The firing grew, and Smalley's exposed fighters fled, scattered, yelled into the growing din, and kept moving, whirling away, making elusive targets.

John twisted to see Cleve still upright, apparently fascinated and horrified both. "Get over in the shadows!" he yelled. "Dammit, Cleve . . . !"

But the clerk turned and hastened toward the rear door, and John watched him, fearfully expecting Cleve's terror to drive him out into the yard where danger lay. But Cleve stopped and peered outside, then moved stealthily to one side of the opening, kneeled and held up the shotgun. When it went off the whole building reverberated. Somewhere a man screamed and others cursed.

"Flanked!" John yelled to Franklin and Herb. "They're out in back, too!"

Franklin nodded without attempting to answer above the bedlam of guns and men, but Herb did. He said: "That blunderbuss'll keep 'em back, by God."

The sniper on the roof was firing from a high angle and his slugs burned deeply into the barn at a murderous angle. John could hear them tearing into the packed earth of the runway. He pressed farther into the gloom, watching for a chance, and when it came, his hands tightened upon the carbine, but he hesitated, didn't fire.

"Herb?"

"Yes?"

"The left-hand gunman you want. . . ."

"Where?"

"Up there on the roof behind the false front."

"Are you sure? How'd you know?"

"I know him."

"All right," Herb said, and, pressing himself flat upon the churned runway, began to edge outward a little. His father called to him sharply.

"Don't expose yourself, Herb!"

But Herb kept on edging out a little, until he could see the roof line across the way, then he held his six-gun with both hands, elbows firmly upon the earth, and waited.

John saw the slanting blast of gunfire smash woodwork and

163

glass across the way and knew Tom's men farther southward were finding targets. For the time being he knew of only one man to oppose and Herb had his loft under sights.

Waiting, John heard men calling to one another beyond vision, southward. He was wondering if it was Tom fighting his way northward along the plank walk when Herb fired and John's ears rang.

The sniper on the roof cried out, and for a moment his carbine was silhouetted against the blood-red sky, then it fell, and Herb was twisting to call out when three slamming shots came from overhead.

Herb let off a startled sound and his supported gun wobbled briefly.

John threw up the carbine, waiting for the Texan to show himself. He didn't, and Herb's father was talking to Herb in a quiet way.

"You winged him, Son, now get back a ways. Where'd he hit you?"

"I don't think he did," Herb said without obeying. "Just one more shot."

He got it when John squeezed off his own shot, and the Texan straightened up, head and shoulders showing, balanced there in plain view with his unfired handgun hanging. Herb shot twice in rapid succession. The Texan broke in the middle and fell forward, crashed down upon the overhang above Murphy's Emporium, rolled a little, and tumbled off the edge into the dust, a great bubble of which puffed skyward under the impact of his body.

Staring, Herb said: "He *is* left-handed, Paw, see?"

"Yes, I see. Now get back here."

A thunderous voice from out back said: "Drop it, you . . . !" And curse words as bitter as gall rang out.

John leaped up, turned, and started back where Cleve still

kneeled, shaking as though with fever. The clerk looked up once. John was shocked by his face and went low beside him.

"Did you get one?"

"I don't know. Someone screamed."

"Is Tom out there . . . or some of the others?"

Cleve wagged his head. "I don't know who is out there, just guns," he said, "and men."

John listened. Most of the firing still seemed to come from out front. He thought the preponderance of it came from the south, down toward the stage office, and that was puzzling, for unless Tom had split up his force, who would be out back ordering others to throw their guns down? But—and it bothered him—the amount of firing southward didn't sound any less now than it had originally, so Tom must not have split up his men. Then who . . . ?

Up front a thunderous fusillade erupted. Cleve started beside him. John leaped up and hastened forward, keeping well along the stalls. Bullets sprayed down through the runway searchingly. He turned long enough to yell for Cleve to flatten against the wall and continued on until he found Franklin Bosworth. The old man's face was twisted with intense concentration. Thirty years seemed to have dropped away from him.

"They're going to storm us, John."

But if that had been the intention of Smalley's men, they were discouraged by a withering and sustained fire from the south. John could hear the bullets slashing woodwork above Jameson's body in the doorway. He smiled to himself. No sane man would try to brave that storm of lead to get inside the barn.

The noise slackened a little. John darted to the opposite side of the barn in time to see Jeff Smalley dash from his saloon almost into the arms of a stalking man whose gray dust-streaked apparel and face made him blend into the dullness of failing

165

light. John threw up the carbine when Smalley slashed downward with his gun at the stranger, who twisted away from the vicious blow. Then there was a muffled explosion and John, stunned, lowered his carbine to see.

Smalley's body went violently backward, crumpled, and hung half on, half off the plank walk. His hat rolled; his gun fell into the dirt.

The dusty man scarcely spent a second look on Smalley. He raised an arm and swung it forward as though throwing something. Immediately other men appeared across the way and realization came numbingly to John that whoever the stranger was, he had more men on Smalley's side of the road and was beckoning them on.

Cleve let go a shattering blast with the shotgun and someone outside yelled at the top of his lungs. "I give up! I give up!"

Franklin Bosworth was standing loosely, face creased into craggy wonder. Herb was on one knee, gun dangling, head twisted backward toward the rear. "What the hell . . . ?" he wondered, and let it trail off.

John lowered the carbine, bewildered.

Out in the roadway a springy figure flashed past, a blurred, lean face pinched up with concentration showed very briefly, then his attention was drawn to four men prodding a very tall, thin man along, with pistols. The sheriff.

John stood up, watching.

Tom Bosworth's thunderous voice yelled out. It was unmistakable and boomingly clear. "Paw, Herb, John? You fellows still in there?"

Herb called back. "Yeah, where are you, Tom?"

"I'm coming. Just stand fast."

The firing became less. It had moved north of the barn, and John thought it must be concentrating itself over by the public corral. There wasn't much cover there, he knew, and if there

166

were horses in the corral, they would be panicky, making shooting accurately just about impossible.

Herb touched his arm lightly. "Something going on," he said. "There's two fellows back there by Cleve in plain sight. They've got their arms in the air."

"Tom . . . ?" John inquired.

"Naw, you heard him. Tom's out front."

"Maybe he split . . . ," John began. "Say, see those fellows prodding the law along? Who the hell are they? Do you know?"

Herb craned his neck, was silent for a long time, until his father walked over, punching spent casings out of his handgun and shoving new cartridges into the cylinder. Then Herb turned to look at the older man. "Those fellows there behind the sheriff, do you recognize any of them, Paw?"

Franklin looked long and hard and shook his head. "Nope, they're strangers to me."

Cleve interrupted their wonderment with an inarticulate sound. John whirled, saw the silhouette in the doorway. Herb and Franklin were also turning. Herb's gun was leaping up when Cleve's voice triggered John.

"Jack!"

The name prompted action, and John knocked Herb's gun aside. Franklin's pistol was cocked, riding lightly but waiting. It was the virtue of his inherent quietude that kept him from firing, the ability to split seconds, use one half for thought, one half for action, and successfully.

John trotted the length of the barn toward the wispy figure. "Lord!" he exclaimed.

Jack's face creased into a frosty smile. "Anyone hurt in here?"

Cleve shuddered to his feet. Very solemnly he said: "No one's hurt, but I know one person whose nerves are ruined for life."

Jack strode into the gloom with his teeth showing. "It took a bit of doing," he told John, "for I'm the last man who'd figure to ride with U.S. marshals, but after I got down there, John, I got to figuring. I knew Jeff pretty blamed well, you'll recall, and I kind of thought I knew you. Well, the upshot was, I figured Jeff'd best you, boy, so, whether we got the contract or not, I reckoned it'd be better to eke along on the passenger trade than lose out altogether, which we'd have done, y'see, if Jeff had you killed and me too scared to come back." Jack wagged his head. "Going into that marshal's office was just about the most uncomfortable thing I ever did in my life."

Herb and his father came up, nodded at Jack, and holstered their guns. John introduced them. There was a brief touching of hands, then Jack said: "Chet's lying out in the road. . . ."

"Herb, here, got him," John said. "He was on top of the building across the way."

"And Jeff. . . . I saw that. He took a swipe at a deputy marshal." In feigned sadness Jack shook his head again. "Too bad, of course, when a man shows that kind of judgment . . . well. . . ."

"Jameson's out there in the roadway, up front," John said. "Smalley shot him. I saw him do it over the doors of the Running Horse."

Jack looked briefly astonished, then shrugged. "Who's left?" he asked.

"Smalley's hammerheads, as far as I know," Herb said. "Have you seen the others? I've got two brothers out there somewhere."

"Those'd be Eb and Tom, wouldn't they?" Jack said. "Sure, they're over by the public corral, trussing up some Christmas geese."

"Safe to go out there now?" Franklin asked, and when Jack nodded, he and Herb started out through the doorway and into the heavy dusk that was descending.

Cleve went in search of a drink of water, trailing the burly scatter-gun, and John groped for his tobacco sack. Jack was grinning at him.

"I suppose I got to ride back to Raton now," he said. "I'm getting so the sight of a saddle makes my rear-end ache."

Over the cigarette John asked: "Didn't the lawmen recognize you?"

"Nope, but y'see, John, I'm not that well known. The only real danger to my hide was Jeff . . . and I'll tell you I felt no sadness when he got it. We're in the clear."

"If that's all I had to worry about," John replied, "I'd be singing."

"What about the seven thousand?"

"Your friend, Cantrell, was responsible for that, only now I don't imagine anyone'll ever prove it."

"So Bosworth loses his seven thousand."

"Not so's you'd notice it. He got a bill of sale out of Jameson before Jameson got killed. He's said he'd forget the seven thousand for Jameson's half interest."

"I see." Jack reached for the sack and papers, began twisting up a cigarette. "Now then, about Bosworth's horses . . . ?"

"I agreed to repay him at the rate of a hundred dollars a month."

Jack worked in silence until he had the cigarette going, then he fixed an odd little smile upon John. "Now that's real nice," he said. "We wouldn't want our partner cheated out of the horses *you stole from me!*"

They both smiled.

Jack said: "I suppose I'm the only one's going to lose out on that deal."

"Well, but it serves you right," John said, "you stole them."

Jack looked up with a wide-eyed expression, almost said something, then didn't, just looked exaggeratedly forlorn and smoked in silence for a moment. "I got a trade to offer you then," he said. "You make the ride down to Raton for that cussed bidding this time, and I'll forget about the horses . . . and the money you owe me."

"I'd do it in a minute," John said, "but for one thing."

"I suppose now you got a wound you just remembered."

"More serious than that. I've got a girl I have to see."

And he left Jack, crossed through the gathering dark and walked heavily northward along the dingy, acrid-smelling atmosphere on the east side of the roadway. He walked as far as the Porters' place, through the gate, up to the porch where she and her father were sitting.

" 'Evening," he said.

The judge nodded at him, and Joyce ignored the greeting to search for signs of bandages.

"It's all over, I guess," John said.

Judge Porter arose from his rocking chair. "The Bosworths?" he asked.

"Unhurt. There were a few casualties, but I didn't stay down there to look at who they were. I probably wouldn't have known them if I had."

"I see. And Smalley and Jameson?"

"Casualties," John said.

The judge said it again: "I see. Well, if you'll excuse me, I suppose I'd best walk down there." He passed John on the steps.

Joyce stood up. Her dress was white and made a cloudy shadow, full and long, against the background of the house. She gazed at him a long time, then said something practical but not appropriate. "Are you hungry, John?"

"I expect I am," he said, moving across the porch to her.

"Then let's eat. I've had two places set for the last hour and no one to fill them." She turned at the doorway. "And I'm hungrier than a bear, tonight."

He threw his hat upon a porch chair, and followed her into the house.

ABOUT THE AUTHOR

Lauran Paine who, under his own name and various pseudonyms has written over a thousand books, was born in Duluth, Minnesota. His family moved to California when he was at a young age and his apprenticeship as a Western writer came about through the years he spent in the livestock trade, rodeos, and even motion pictures where he served as an extra because of his expert horsemanship in several films starring movie cowboy Johnny Mack Brown. In the late 1930s, Paine trapped wild horses in northern Arizona and even, for a time, worked as a professional farrier. Paine came to know the Old West through the eyes of many who had been born in the previous century, and he learned that Western life had been very different from the way it was portrayed on the screen. "I knew men who had killed other men," he later recalled. "But they were the exceptions. Prior to and during the Depression, people were just too busy eking out an existence to indulge in Saturday-night brawls." He served in the U.S. Navy in the Second World War and began writing for Western pulp magazines following his discharge. It is interesting to note that all of his earliest novels (written under his own name and the pseudonym Mark Carrel) were published in the British market and he soon had as strong a following in that country as in the United States. Paine's Western fiction is characterized by strong plots, authenticity, an apparently effortless ability to construct situation and character, and a preference for building his stories upon a solid foundation of historical fact. *Adobe Empire* (1956), one of his best early novels, is a fictionalized account of the last twenty years in the life of trader William Bent and, in an off-trail way, has a melancholy, bittersweet texture that is not easily forgotten. In later novels like *Cache Cañon* (Five Star Westerns, 1998) and *Halfmoon Ranch* (Five Star Westerns, 2007), he showed that the special magic and power of his stories and characters had only matured along with his basic themes of changing times, changing attitudes, learning from experience, respecting Nature, and the yearning for a simpler, more moderate way of life.